GHOST TROUBLE

*Also available by Pete Johnson,
and published by Corgi Yearling Books:*

PHANTOM FEAR
'Another fine book from Pete Johnson'
School Librarian

EYES OF THE ALIEN
'Very readable and skillfully plotted'
Observer

THE FRIGHTENERS
'Prepare to be thoroughly spooked'
Daily Mail

TRAITOR
'Fast-paced and energetic'
The Bookseller

AVENGER
'A brilliant read'
Sunday Express

TRUST ME, I'M A TROUBLEMAKER
'The devastatingly funny Pete Johnson'
Sunday Times

RESCUING DAD
'Most buoyant, funny and optimistic'
Carousel

HOW TO TRAIN YOUR PARENTS
'Makes you laugh out loud'
Sunday Times

HELP! I'M A CLASSROOM GAMBLER
'A real romp of a read'
Achuka

PETE JOHNSON

GHOST TROUBLE

Corgi Yearling Books

GHOST TROUBLE
A CORGI YEARLING BOOK : 978 0 440 87125 5

First published in Great Britain as separate editions by Corgi Yearling
an imprint of Random House Children's Books

THE GHOST DOG first published 1996
THE CREEPER first published 2000

This edition published 2006

3 5 7 9 10 8 6 4

Corgi Yearling Books are published by Random House Children's
Books,
61–63 Uxbridge Road, London W5 5SA,
a division of The Random House Group Ltd,
Addresses for companies within the Random House Group Limited can be
found at: www.randomhouse.co.uk/offices.htm

THE RANDOM HOUSE GROUP Limited Reg. No. 954009
www.kidsatrandomhouse.co.uk

A CIP catalogue record for this book
is available from the British Library

The Random House Group Limited supports The Forest Stewardship
Council® (FSC®), the leading international forest-certification organisation.
Our books carrying the FSC label are printed on FSC®-certified paper.
FSC is the only forest-certification scheme supported by the leading
environmental organisations, including Greenpeace. Our
paper procurement policy can be found at
www.randomhouse.co.uk/environment

Printed and bound in Great Britain by Clays Ltd, St Ives plc

THE GHOST DOG

Illustrated by Peter Dennis

The Ghost Dog is dedicated to
Jan, Linda, Robin and Harry;
Rose, Jack and Freddie Jewitt;
Jo and Laura May;
Alex and Grant Harnett

With grateful thanks.

CHAPTER ONE

The first time I only saw its face.

Out of the darkness it came floating towards me.

It had evil red eyes.

Blood poured out of its mouth.

It was the ugliest, most horrible thing I had ever seen.

And I'd brought it to life.

I'd thought it was only mad scientists in stories who could create monsters. Not ten-year-old boys like me: Daniel Grant.

Don't ask me how I did it. I'm still not sure. I certainly never meant it to appear at my spooky party.

*　　*　　*

It was Laura's idea to have a party for Halloween.

She first mentioned it after school when we were taking Rocky for a walk. Rocky is my pet rat.

At first I'd wanted a dog but my mum wouldn't let me. So then I went to the pet shop and saw this albino rat in a cage. And he looked at me so imploringly I knew he wanted me to buy him. So I did. Now I reckon he's the best pet you can have.

Every day after school he snuggles down my shirt while Laura and I take him to the common. There we let him run around. He loves that but he never tries to get away. In fact, he can be a bit of a pain because he wants to be stroked all the time.

Rocky was licking orange off our fingers when I started yawning again.

'You've been yawning all day,' said Laura.

'I know,' I said. 'It's because . . .' I hesitated. I didn't want to tell anyone and yet I did. Perhaps I would just tell Laura.

By the way, people are always calling Laura my girlfriend and I know they say it as a kind of joke but it really annoys me.

Laura and I often go fishing as well as kick-boxing every Wednesday. She's an excellent goal-keeper and never seems to mind being the only girl when we play football. In fact, I think she likes it. She's quite small with dark brown hair and a quiet whispery voice, although she can shout when she wants to. She's my best mate and she has been ever since we met at infant school.

So then I told her. 'You know on the news they said about that man who'd escaped from prison?'

'The one with the really mean face,' began Laura.

'That's him,' I said. 'Well, I didn't get

much sleep last night because I kept hearing these noises and I was sure he was hiding in my attic.'

Laura's eyes grew bigger. 'And what was it?'

'Rocky jumping up and down in his cage,' I replied. 'At least I think that's what it was.' We both laughed nervously, then I started stroking Rocky. 'When I was younger, a lot younger,' I went on, 'I used to arrange my toy soldiers so that all their guns were pointing at the door. Then some nights I'd put my tanks out too . . . I still like to have something by my bed even if it's only a tennis racket, just in case.' I paused.

There was silence for a moment before Laura said, quietly, 'What I hate is when that man at the end of *Crimewatch* says, "Sleep well tonight and don't have any bad dreams, will you?" And I think, it's all right for you in your nice, comfy studio with about two hundred people around you, but I'm on my own upstairs . . . some nights I'll be thinking about what he's said so much, that I have to go and switch my light on and stand in the light for a little while.' She shivered and smiled. 'It's Halloween next week.'

'I know.'

'We must do something,' she said. 'And not trick or treat. Last year everyone was doing that. No, we ought to have a proper party where we can play *Murder in the Dark.*'

'I love *Murder in the Dark,*' I cried.

'And afterwards we could all sit round and tell really gory stories,' she said. We looked at each other excitedly. Then Laura sighed. 'Only my dad would never let me have a party like that.'

I silently agreed. Laura's dad's all right but he gets stressed very easily. Like yesterday, he made Laura go up to her room just because he found her shoes down by the sofa.

'There's always my house,' I said.

'Do you think your mum would let you?' asked Laura.

'It depends what sort of mood she's in, but I think I can talk her round, especially if I get Roy on my side.' Roy is my mum's boyfriend.

But in the end I didn't need Roy's support. To my total surprise Mum said 'Yes', rightaway.

'How many friends can I invite?' I asked.

'About six,' suggested Mum.

'Not counting Laura.'

Mum smiled. 'Not counting Laura . . . and we'll have to keep an eye on Carrie. We don't want her getting scared.'

Carrie is my seven-year-old sister. 'Nothing scares her,' I said.

Next day Laura and I worked out who we were going to invite. Top of both our lists was Harry, because he's mad. He really is. I mean, I've never seen anyone laugh like Harry. He's got this really loud laugh and when he starts he just can't stop: tears fall down his face and he always leans too far back on his chair and falls over. Then, because he's laughing so much he can't get up again, which winds teachers up something rotten. It's brilliant to see.

Next to Laura, Harry is probably my best mate. He got really excited about the Halloween party. So did everyone else we invited. Then, two days before Halloween, came shock news.

'I know you're going to be disappointed,' said Mum, 'but I'm afraid we're going to have to cancel the Halloween party.'

I looked up sharply. 'Why?'

Mum became embarrassed. 'Well, Roy's

been offered this job which means he'll be away on business a lot in America over the next few months, so he's asked if Aaron could stay here with us and make a fresh start.'

Aaron is Roy's son. I'd only seen him about twice but that was enough. He just loves himself; a total bighead. Mum went rattling on. 'So Aaron will be moving in on Friday

night. I know that's when we'd planned your party but I can't manage a party on that night as well. Don't worry, though, I will make it up to you.'

'Don't bother,' I muttered.

'Oh come on, Dan, we'll do something special soon, I promise,' said Mum. 'Got any ideas?'

14

'Yeah, a Halloween party,' I said. 'That's all I want.'

I was so angry about my party being cancelled it was only later I realized what else it meant: my home was going to be invaded. By Aaron.

Ever since my dad walked out, it had just been my mum, Carrie and me and I'd got to like that. I certainly didn't want it changed now.

'Why has Aaron got to come here?' I demanded. 'Why can't he go to his nan's or ...'

'Because I want to do this for Roy,' interrupted Mum. 'It's a decision I've made and that's that.' She had a real 'Don't argue with me' look on her face. Then she added, a bit more gently, 'It is the right thing to do. Later you'll see that.'

She was smiling at me now. I turned away. Then I thought of something. 'And where's he going to sleep?'

'I can't see him sharing with Carrie, can you?' replied Mum, trying to make a little joke of it all. 'And you have got the biggest bedroom.'

But as I said to Laura later, that doesn't mean Mum can just move someone into my room without even asking me. How would she like it if I told her I was bunging another woman into her bedroom.

'She wouldn't like it at all,' agreed Laura. 'And I'd really hate to share my room with a stranger,' she added.

'This Aaron's ruined everything,' I said, 'including our Halloween party.'

It was about half-past-seven on Halloween night when Roy and Aaron arrived in this big van. The first thing Aaron unpacked was this new mountain bike, which his dad had just bought for him. I think I'm lucky if my dad sends me a five-pound gift token at Christmas.

Then Mum said to me, 'Show your guest where he's staying.'

I wanted to say, 'He's not my guest,' but I didn't, as earlier Mum had given me this pep talk. 'Now, you must make Aaron feel welcome: remember, his mum's passed away and it can't be easy for him, new home, new school . . .' So I did try and twist my face into a smile as I went up the stairs with him. But watching him pile his suitcases into my room gave me this really tight pain in my stomach.

Aaron prowled around my room and didn't look at all impressed. He pointed at Rocky in his cage. 'You've got a pet rat.' He sounded mocking.

'He's called Rocky – and he lives here,' I added, in case Aaron was going to say he couldn't share a room with a pet rat.

But instead, Aaron picked up the scarf I'd put on top of the bunk bed – just so he'd know that was my place. 'So you're a Spurs supporter,' he said.

'Yeah, what about you?'

'Arsenal is the only team worth supporting.' He turned around and glared at me. He'd had his hair shaved really short round the sides; I think he was trying to look hard. But he was actually very skinny and quite small, half a head smaller than me, even though he was a year older.

Then Mum, Roy and Carrie all tumbled into my room.

'Getting settled in all right, Aaron?' asked my mum. 'Daniel's made space for you, so there should be plenty of room.'

'Oh yes, plenty of room,' said Roy, rubbing his hands together. Then he laughed loudly, showing all his white pointy teeth. He had his arm all round Mum's shoulder. I hate it when seriously old people do things like that.

At first Carrie was skipping around him excitedly. But later, when we were all sitting downstairs having sandwiches, she just sat on Mum's lap, not talking to anyone. Aaron and I didn't say much either.

It was just Mum and Roy who were babbling away. Roy was wearing his usual leather jacket and jeans. He rides a Harley Davidson motorbike and has taken me out on it a few times. I guess he's pretty good to me, although he's never bought me a mountain bike. He said to me, 'I'm sorry you had to postpone your Halloween party.'

'It doesn't matter,' I said, quietly.

'Yes, it does,' said Roy, firmly. 'We're still going to have it, you know.'

'A Halloween party has to be on Halloween,' I muttered.

'OK, well, we'll just call it something else, like . . .'

I looked up. 'A spooky party.'

'Brilliant,' he said. 'And we'll make this party even scarier than Halloween. We can get some plastic skeletons from the joke shop and some masks and . . .'

'When?' I interrupted.

Roy turned to Mum. 'I'm back from the States two weeks tonight, so how about holding it then?'

She nodded, smiling. 'Why not?' She turned to Aaron. 'Do you like spooky parties?'

Aaron just shrugged and looked bored.

'Of course he does,' said his dad, heartily. 'Make out some proper invitations, Daniel,' he went on: 'After all, everyone has Halloween parties but spooky parties are much more special.'

'We'll do the invitations tomorrow,' I said. 'Me and Laura,' I added, just in case anyone thought I'd meant me and Aaron.

Next morning I woke up very early. And straightaway I heard it, the noise which had been waking me up all night: Aaron breathing really noisily and deeply through his mouth. It was as if he were trying to suck up all the air in my bedroom, leaving none for me.

INVITATION
BE THERE OR BEWARE

IT'S SPOOKY PARTY NIGHT

ENJOY THE FRIGHT

AT: DANIEL'S CRYPT
ALSO KNOWN AS
22 WOODSIDE ROAD

ON:
FRIDAY 14TH NOVEMBER

TIME: 7 O'CLOCK

WARNING:
NOT FOR THE FAINT-HEARTED.

I crept down the ladder from my bed. At least I still had the top bunk. Then I went over to Rocky's cage. At once he was pressing his nose through the cage, eager to say 'Hello'. I let him lick my fingers while whispering to him. Then I turned around and saw I was being watched. Aaron was sitting up in bed, staring at me without saying anything.

'All right?' I muttered.

'All right,' he muttered back. And that was all we said until I fled to the bathroom.

Mum thought Aaron and I were going to walk to school together. But as soon as we got out of the front door we set off on opposite sides of the road. Luckily he wasn't in the same class as me. At lunchtime I saw him on the back field with some guys from his class, but he totally ignored me.

At home we pretty much ignored each other too. Mum remarked about how quiet he was. 'You'd hardly know he was here,' she said. Yet, he was here: watching television and continually flicking the channels to teletext; leaving his clothes and his shoes and hair gel all over my room; cluttering up the house with his mountain bike; and, worst of all, he had a way of looking at me which I came to hate: somehow he could put me down without saying a word.

Then, the day before my spooky party, Aaron did something which really infuriated me. I'd had to leave school early to go to the dentist. So it was after five o'clock when I finally called round at Laura's. To my surprise Harry was there too, and for once he wasn't smiling. Both he and Laura looked very serious.

'What's the matter with you two?' I asked.

'Nothing, only . . .' began Harry. Then he looked at Laura. 'Come on, we've got to tell him.'

'Tell me what?' I cried.

'After school today,' started Laura, 'we went to McDonald's and Aaron was there with some boys from his class . . .'

'He was showing off so much I wanted to punch him,' interrupted Harry.

'What was he saying?' I asked.

'Oh, just going on and on about all the things he'd done. I didn't really listen,' said Harry, dismissively. 'But then he came over to Laura and me and said he'd buy us both Big Macs if we liked.'

I stared at him disbelievingly. 'He did what?'

'And he was all smiles,' said Laura. 'Kept going on about how he had the money so it was no trouble.'

I clenched my hands into fists. At once I knew what Aaron's game was: he was trying to steal my friends away from me. 'So what did you do?' I asked, my voice starting to shake.

'We said no, of course,' said Harry. 'We didn't want anything from him. He's just a show-off.'

'You can't buy friends,' added Laura, softly.

I shot her a grateful look, but then I started thinking about Aaron again. 'I really hate people like him,' I whispered, fiercely, 'who are just so full of themselves, they try and take over everything.'

'He deserves a lesson,' said Harry.

I looked at Laura and Harry, then said, slowly, 'At the spooky party tomorrow, we've got to scare him . . .'

'Yeah,' cried Harry at once.

'And we won't just scare him a bit,' I continued. 'Let's give him the biggest shock of his life.'

CHAPTER TWO

It was at seven o'clock I turned into a zombie: a zombie who has just been woken from the dead and isn't too happy about it.

Mum put fake blood all over my face and we found some really old raggy clothes. Then I sprayed this cobweb stuff over me. I thought I looked pretty good, actually.

Then Laura and Harry turned up. Harry was a werewolf: he had a brilliant mask with hair all coming off it and on his left hand he was wearing this furry glove which looked just like a claw. While Laura had come as a hunchback: she'd made her face very pale, put dust over some old clothes and, of course, she had a cushion up her back.

'You three do look a state,' said Mum. We took this as a huge compliment.

'What do you think of Laura, then?' I asked Harry.

'A big improvement,' he said. 'Actually, I really wanted to come as a poltergeist.'

'But how would you have done that?' asked Laura.

'Don't know,' said Harry. 'That's why I didn't come as one.' He began to laugh.

'You're mad,' said Laura.

'That's true,' he agreed.

Then the front door opened and Aaron shot up the stairs, carrying a large package.

'What's he got in there?' asked Harry.

I shrugged my shoulders.

'Go and have a look; after all, he's in your room,' said Harry.

'No, I don't want to make him feel too important,' I replied.

A couple of minutes later we all saw what was in the parcel: Aaron sauntered back down the stairs in this brand new Spiderman costume. He started strutting over to us.

'That must have cost a bomb,' exclaimed Harry.

And Mum said to Roy, 'I thought the children were making their own costumes for this party.'

'Oh, I'd promised Aaron a Spiderman costume ages ago,' replied Roy. 'It's just, tonight, I finally got round to buying it. Doesn't he look great?'

Mum didn't answer, instead, she charged back into the kitchen. Roy rushed after her, while Aaron just stood there as if frozen to the spot.

'Look at him,' I muttered. 'He thinks he's so great.'

'It's much better to make your own costume,' said Laura.

'Of course it is,' I said. Yet I couldn't help thinking how shabby and cheap my costume looked against Aaron's. His was a deluxe costume; mine looked as if it was out of the bargain basement.

'It's a cheat buying a costume,' I cried, loud enough for Aaron to hear. 'He shouldn't be allowed into my party like that.'

Aaron took a couple of steps towards me. 'I see you've come as yourself,' he hissed. 'An idiot.'

'Ignore him,' whispered Laura.

But I was already squaring up to him.

'What about you,' I taunted. 'Daddy's little pet.'

Now we were facing each other just as if we were about to have a fight. I really think there would have been a fight if Roy hadn't burst in, yelling, 'Come on everyone, let's get busy. We haven't long to make this house scary, you know.'

So we charged about putting black sheeting over the porch, hanging up a skeleton just inside the doorway and changing the light in the hallway to orange, as that was spookier. Then Mum, who had taken Carrie off to stay with a friend, returned and Roy kept smiling at her and asking her what she thought of everything.

Soon the guests started arriving, shouting and giggling excitedly in their masks. Then Roy organized some games like apple bobbing and eating a doughnut off a piece of string, and the treasure hunt.

For the treasure hunt we had to go out into the garden and find these bags of gold coins which Mum and Roy had hooked on to the bushes and trees. 'Remember the pond is

31

out of bounds,' Mum called after us. Last time we'd played this game, someone had fallen in the pond. It was so funny.

We tore around the garden in twos and threes. Only Aaron was on his own. Everyone was whispering about him though, and what a 'big show-off' he was, wearing that Spiderman costume tonight.

'So when are we going to scare Aaron?' asked Harry.

'After tea, when we play *Murder in the Dark*, and there are no grown-ups around,' I said. 'We'll do something, then, for sure.'

But I still wasn't certain what, exactly. We trooped back inside for tea. There were burgers with lots of ketchup on, which I called 'Blood Burgers', spider cakes which had icing in the shape of a spider's web on top, jellies with plastic spiders in them . . . there was just so much food. The only trouble was it took such a long time to eat, that by the time we'd finished it was almost the end of the party.

'I don't think we've got enough time to play *Murder in the Dark*,' said Mum.

But I was determined. 'We've got to play

Murder in the Dark, haven't we?' I cried. I looked at Harry and Laura, who immediately backed me up. And soon the whole party was chanting: 'We want *Murder in the Dark*. We want *Murder in the Dark*.'

'All right,' said Mum, finally. 'Everyone into the lounge.'

We huddled around Mum and Roy. Mum took out this pack of cards. 'Now, I'm going to pass the cards around. Don't, whatever you do, turn your card over yet.' There was a tense silence as Mum handed around the cards. 'Now you may turn your card over,' she said. 'Remember, whoever gets the Ace of Spades is the murderer.'

I gazed at my card with a mixture of astonishment and excitement.

For the first time ever, I had the Ace of Spades.

'Who has got the Ace of Spades?' asked my mum.

'I have,' I cried, holding the card right up in the air.

'Then tonight you are the murderer,' said Mum, handing me the rubber dagger. I grinned around while my heart was thumping wildly. I saw Laura and Harry looking eagerly at me. And I knew what they were thinking: get Aaron.

No-one ever wants to be the first person caught: it's like saying, 'I'm a geek.' So I was determined to catch Aaron first tonight.

'Now you've all got just five minutes to hide from our murderer.'

I gave an evil laugh while twisting the dagger around in my hand. 'You've all got five minutes to live.'

'Just one last thing,' said Mum. 'The hall light has to be left on at all times, all right?' Everyone nodded solemnly. 'Right, then, off you go,' she cried. And at once everyone

34

rushed off, Harry and Laura giving me another look as they left.

'Just listen to them,' grinned Roy. And it did sound as if there was a herd of mad rhinos charging about upstairs – only rhinos who kept laughing and yelling hysterically.

Mum looked at her stop-watch. 'Two minutes left,' she called. The sounds upstairs were quieter and more muffled now.

'Hey, why don't we join in this?' cried Roy suddenly.

'Well, we've only fifty-four seconds left,' said Mum.

'That's plenty of time,' grinned Roy and with that he grabbed Mum's hand and they rushed away, Mum handing me the stopwatch as she left.

I watched Mum and Roy race up the stairs. Then, by a piece of good fortune, I glimpsed someone else run downstairs. Aaron.

But I played fair. I turned my back and counted off the last seconds on the stopwatch.

So Aaron was hiding downstairs. I wondered where he'd go. And then I was certain I knew: he'd hide in the laundry basket under the stairs.

For that's where I used to hide. It was a bit smelly in that laundry basket, especially if any of my old socks were in there. But it was a superb hiding place, and no-one ever looked there. No doubt Aaron thought he was really clever thinking of it. Well, I'd soon wipe the smug smile off his face.

Time was up. My first idea was just to charge over to the laundry basket. But then

I decided, to add atmosphere, I'd switch the hall light off first. I know Mum had said to keep the light on, but I wanted to really scare Aaron.

So I switched off the orange light, then stared around me, letting my eyes get used to the darkness. It suddenly seemed to get colder. I shivered. And then I saw it creeping towards me. It looked like a large dog or something. It must be someone on their hands and knees.

Aaron.

He's realized I'm on to his hiding place and is trying to sneak past me.

All at once I charged forward with my rubber dagger . . . and then let out the most

37

terrible cry of pain you've ever heard. For I'd tripped over something and fallen splat on to my face. As I tried to get up this terrible pain shot up from my ankle. As I wobbled to my feet the pain became sharper. I let out another cry. I couldn't help it. Then I heard a door burst open and Roy calling down the stairs: 'What's going on down there?' At that same moment the doorbell rang.

Footsteps raced downstairs and I heard my mum's voice exclaiming: 'Who switched the light out? I know the switch is around here somewhere,' while the doorbell rang again, twice this time.

Then all at once the hall was full of orange light again and Mum, Roy, and two very worried-looking parents were all staring at me.

'I fell over,' I gasped, looking downwards at the box in which we'd put all the rubbish from the party. 'I fell over a box,' I added helpfully.

'I told you to leave that hall light on,' cried Mum. I had a feeling this wouldn't be the last time I'd hear her say that tonight.

Now everyone was jostling downstairs to

see what was happening: and what was happening was me feeling more than a bit stupid.

Just before I hobbled away to the kitchen with Mum I watched 'Spiderman' slowly clamber out of the laundry basket.

I gaped at him incredulously. It can't have been Aaron I'd spotted in the darkness.

So who or what was it?

I shivered again.

CHAPTER THREE

'I told you not to switch the hall light off . . . but as usual, you have to go your own way. Well, what happened serves you right.'

'Number four,' I murmured to myself. There was no point in arguing with Mum; that only got her even madder. And besides, she was right; it was my own fault. So all I could do was keep score of the number of times Mum nagged me while she strapped up my ankle.

Would she top her all-time record of seven 'nags' in one hour? Not tonight. In fact, when she saw me limping around the kitchen she threw away the record and said, 'You're not a bad boy really, just a bit headstrong. It's a shame your party had to end like that.' Then to cheer me up she said I could go out to the hut in the garden with Laura and Harry (they were sleeping over; all my other guests had gone home long ago) and tell scary stories.

I popped upstairs to get Rocky. Aaron was there, lying on the bottom bunk in his Spiderman outfit. I just wanted to go over to him and punch him in the face. I had a feeling he wanted to do the same to me. But instead, we totally ignored each other. Then I ran downstairs and went out to the hut at the bottom of the garden where Laura and Harry were already waiting for me. It was pitch dark in there except for the light from the torch which Mum had given Harry. Rocky jumped on to Laura's shoulder and started cleaning himself.

It was quite a small hut which reeked of mustiness and stale grass from the lawn-mower in the corner. There was just one tiny window patterned with cobwebs. I squashed down between Laura – who was now sitting

on her hump – and Harry. Then, before anyone else could say it, I declared, 'I made a
right fool of myself tonight.'

'That's true,' said Harry, grinning at me.

'And we certainly scared Aaron, didn't
we?' sighed Laura.

'All right, all right,' I muttered. 'I really
thought he was . . . it was so weird.'

'What was?' asked Laura.

'When I switched the hall light off, I saw
this shape moving towards me. At first I
thought it was Aaron on his hands and
knees, and then . . . well it could have been
a dog: a massive dog.'

'Like that Irish wolfhound we used to see,' said Harry. 'Remember it?'

'Oh yes,' cried Laura. 'It used to terrify me it was so big. It would suddenly tear out of those flats by the school.'

'And its owner was this really little guy,' said Harry. 'We used to say that dog was his bodyguard.'

'Too right,' I said. 'No-one would mess with that dog, yank your leg off as soon as look at you, that one. No wonder it always looked so superior.'

'And sometimes we'd hear it behind us,' murmured Laura, 'because it used to breathe really heavily . . . Oh, I was so glad when that man and his dog moved away.'

'Only tonight, it came back,' said Harry, 'as the ghost dog.' He shone the torch right into my face. 'Of course, you could be making this all up.'

'No, I'm not. I swear on your life.'

'On my life,' exclaimed Harry.

'Joke. No, I swear on my life I did see something.'

'We'll believe you,' said Harry. 'Millions wouldn't.' He swung the torch away from me and around the hut. As it alighted on to the door, the handle began to move. I could sense Laura and Harry tensing beside me. Harry kept the torch on the door handle, as it turned again.

'I don't like this,' whispered Laura.

'Maybe it's your ghost dog,' muttered Harry, 'wanting to be taken for walk.' We laughed nervously.

Suddenly the door sprang open and Roy and Aaron were staring in at us. Roy gave one of his hearty laughs. 'Did we scare you then?'

'No, not at all,' said Harry and me.

'Just a bit,' whispered Laura.

'All right if we join you?' asked Roy. I groaned inwardly. But Roy was already squeezing in beside me. As always, he smelt of too much soap.

'Come on, Aaron, room for one more,' called Roy. His tone was light-hearted but it was an order just the same.

Aaron squashed down beside his dad. He looked awkward and angry. He'd changed out of his Spiderman costume and was just wearing his usual T-shirt and jeans now.

'So what are we doing, all telling chilling stories?' Roy winked at us. I liked Roy, he could be a good bloke. But I did think at times he tried too hard to be one of the gang. He didn't seem to realize there were certain events at which adults weren't welcome. And ghost-telling events was one of them.

How could you tell really bloodthirsty, gory tales with a grown-up there?

'Aaron knows some good ghost stories,' began Roy.

'No, I don't,' interrupted Aaron rudely.

'Yes, you do, Aaron. Come on, share them with your friends.'

Aaron glared at his dad. 'Just leave it, all right,' he whispered.

46

Roy stirred angrily and there was an awkward silence until Harry declared, 'Well, I know a spooky story, want to hear it?' Laura, Roy and I nodded eagerly.

'It all began one dark and gloomy night,' said Harry, 'when this woman, who's in the house all on her own, gets a phone call. This really husky voice says to her: "Hello, I am Blood Fingers and I'm coming to get you." The woman put the phone down, shaking. Then a minute later the phone rings again and she hears that horrible, husky voice say, "I am Blood Fingers and I am at your gate." The phone keeps ringing and each time he is getting closer. "I am Blood Fingers and I am in your garden. I am Blood Fingers and I am at your door" and then . . . "I am Blood Fingers and I am in your house and I know where you are. I can see you. I am standing right next to you." The woman turns round and there is this huge guy with blood all over his hands. "Hello," he goes, "I'm Blood Fingers. You haven't got any plasters, have you?" '

At once, Harry burst into peals of laughter. And it was hard not to join in.

Even Aaron laughed faintly.

'You really had me going there,' Roy said to Harry. He grinned broadly.

'Laura's turn now,' joked Harry.

'Oh, I can't think,' began Laura, 'my mind's gone blank. They do say, if at midnight on Halloween night you comb your hair a hundred times, then stare hard into the mirror, you'll see the face of the person you're going to marry.'

'That's not scary,' I said.

'Depends who you see,' said Harry.

'There's a story,' went on Laura, 'that a man did this and then he saw a vampire in his mirror which ripped his face open.'

'Nice,' murmured Harry.

Roy got up. 'I expect I'll be told off if I don't give a hand with the drying-up. So I'll leave you to it. I enjoyed your story, Harry.' Then, in a piercing whisper to Aaron, 'And don't be afraid to join in.'

Even I couldn't help feeling a bit embarrassed for Aaron at that moment. There's nothing worse than a parent who tries to push you into things.

I think Laura felt a bit sorry for Aaron, too, because she said, quite gently to him, 'Would you like to have a go at telling a ghost story now?'

Aaron didn't answer for a moment. Then he said in this really sneery voice, 'I stopped telling ghost stories years ago. They never scared me anyway . . .'

I was so angry I couldn't speak at first. Why did Aaron always have to act as if he was way above us? He ruined everything. Then Harry looked across at me. 'There's one ghost story which scares everyone, isn't there, Dan . . . a true one, too?'

I hadn't a clue what Harry was talking about, but I went along with him. 'Yeah, that's a terrible story, but we'd better not tell Aaron that one; it would only give him nightmares.'

Aaron gave a mocking laugh.

'Will you tell Aaron the story or shall I?' asked Harry.

'I will,' I said. 'This is the true story of . . . of the ghost dog.' And as I said those words, my heart began to beat excitedly. I switched off the torch so the whole place was in darkness.

A picture was forming at the back of my head. And as it became clearer I felt this strange power building up inside me. 'This is an old, local legend,' I began, my voice shaking slightly with excitement. 'There was this boy who lived with his parents and they were quite poor. One night the boy goes downstairs to get some biscuits when he finds a dead dog in his basement.'

'Aaah, that's sad,' murmured Laura.

'But suddenly the dog springs to life, and it's the biggest dog the boy has ever seen: an Irish wolfhound. But he tells the boy not to be afraid, and says: "If you do me a favour I'll do you one. Will you make me a grave where I can rest. If you do that I'll give you a hundred pounds."

'The boy's eyes open wide when he hears about the hundred pounds and he asks for the money rightaway. "All right, I'll trust you," says the dog and he gets the boy to follow him. They walk into the deepest part of the old churchyard and then the dog asks the boy to lift a large stone up. The boy does so and underneath the stone are ten ten-pound notes. The boy stares at the money in amazement. He's never had so much money in his life before.

'"Now I can go to the fair," he cries.

'"Don't forget your part of the bargain," the dog calls after him.

'"No, I'll be back tonight to make your grave, I promise," cries the boy.

'"I'll be here," says the dog and with a little sigh he sits down and waits . . . and waits. But the boy has such a good time at the fair with his mates, that he forgets all about the dog.

'But later that night the boy hears strange scratching noises in his bedroom. And then he sees a pair of red eyes staring at him. It is the dog. "You broke your promise to me," he says. "Now I shall make sure you never forget me. I am going to haunt your dreams for the rest of your life."

'And that is what the dog did. Every night when the boy closed his eyes the dog was waiting for him; and each night the dog became more monstrous and terrifying. Until, one morning, his parents found the boy dead in his bed. And on his face was a look of such terror . . . he had been literally frightened to death by the ghost dog.'

I paused. That story had seemed so real to me I'd lost myself in it, even shuddering at the end. But had it scared Aaron? All at once, there was loud, mocking laughter.

'What a load of old rubbish,' said Aaron.

'It's not rubbish,' I replied fiercely. 'It's real.'

Then Harry said, 'Come on Danny, you haven't told Aaron the end of the story, have you?'

'You tell him the rest, then,' I replied, wondering what Harry was up to.

'Well,' said Harry. 'The end of the story is this: the dog has to go off and make its own grave. It digs a hole, then it carries some stones to cover up the grave. And even though the stones make the dog's mouth bleed, it goes on getting the stones. And finally, the dog finished making his grave, its mouth full of blood. And the dog said that if anyone took so much as one stone away from his grave he would haunt them for ever.'

'And do you know where he is buried?' said Laura, picking up the story now. 'Just up the road by the old church. Of course, I'd be too scared to even move a stone, let alone take one away. That place really gives me the creeps. But ... you wouldn't be scared, would you, Aaron?' Then she added, slyly, 'So why don't you take a stone away?'

'What, now?' whispered Aaron. Suddenly, his voice seemed to have shrunk.

'Yes, why not now?' I said. 'You don't believe in any of it, do you?'

'Go on, I dare you,' said Laura.

'So do I,' joined in Harry.

All three of us stared at him expectantly. We had him cornered. He sat very still as if he were playing statues.

'But we'd never be allowed to go out now,' he said, at last. He was trying to sound tough again, but his voice was shaking all over the place.

'You leave that to me,' I said. 'Now, will you go through with it or do you want to chicken out?'

'I never chicken out of anything,' he whispered.

'Right, well I'll just go and get us permission.' I sprang to my feet, forgetting all about my twisted ankle. The pain made me wince for a moment. Then I limped into the kitchen. Roy was putting some glasses away in the cupboard. He turned and smiled at me.

'How's it all going?' he asked.

'Well, we've been telling Aaron the ghost story about the old church down the road and now he's really keen to see it.'

'What, now?' exclaimed Roy. 'Bit late, isn't it?'

'It's just Aaron's so keen.' And from my tone of voice you'd have thought Aaron and I had become very chummy.

Roy considered for a moment. 'Well, it's good Aaron is joining in at last. I suppose a quick look would be all right. I'll have to come with you, of course, but I'll try not to cramp your style.'

I rushed back to tell the others. Laura and Harry looked really excited; Aaron kept his face blank. But I knew he was getting scared and that made me very happy.

Then Mum appeared. 'I don't think you should go walking on that ankle,' she said.

'It's fine now,' I lied. 'And Roy said we could,' I added. Mum gave Roy one of her looks and muttered about this being a daft time to go out, but she didn't stop us.

The streets were all lit up with pale orange lights, but most of the houses we passed were in darkness. And there was this eerie silence which made my skin tingle.

The path leading to the old church was so narrow we had to walk in single file. At the end of the path was an old gate. It opened with a creaky sigh, and above it was a message. We all peered intently at it thinking it might be something bloodcurdling, like: THIS CHURCHYARD IS HAUNTED. GO ON IF YOU DARE. But it just said: PLEASE CONTROL YOUR DOGS.

'Doesn't say anything about controlling your rats though, does it?' I said. I stole a glance at Rocky who had snuggled down my arm. 'So Rocky, you can go wild tonight if you like.'

Roy shone his torch ahead of him. 'See, there's the church,' he said. And nestling behind all the trees was a grey stone church.

'But this church is positively ancient,' cried Roy, excitedly. 'I don't think I've ever seen such an old church.' He sprang forward with his torch, then turned back when he saw we weren't following him.

'All right if we go off and explore?' I asked.

'Just for a few minutes then,' he said doubtfully, 'but stay in sight.' Then he added, 'This church is a real piece of history, you know.' We nodded politely but didn't follow him.

Laura whispered to me, 'What if there aren't any old stones here?'

'There must be some,' I replied, confidently.

We walked up the gravelly path. 'We should have brought another torch,' I muttered. 'It's really hard to see much.' The trees were swaying majestically above us, and I could hear the long grass stirring in the wind.

Suddenly, Harry called, 'Look at this!' He was pointing at a tree, whose trunk was bent right over. It was really weird. Even Aaron couldn't help staring at it.

'Wind must have caught it,' said Harry.

'It looks as if it's been shot,' said Laura. 'There's something very sad about this tree.' Two lorries rumbled noisily past and for a moment lit up that mysterious tree. That's when we saw what was lying around the tree: hundreds of stones.

'That's the spot,' cried Harry, at once.

'Yeah, that's it all right,' I replied. I couldn't have been more excited if we'd discovered gold. I looked at Aaron. 'This is the spot where the dog made his grave and he said if anyone took so much as a stone away he would haunt them for ever. That's why there are so many stones here. No-one has dared remove one until . . . until . . .' Something was behind me.

A huge shadow.

The shadow spoke. 'Good evening.' I whirled around to see this elderly man out with his dog, a little white terrier.

'Good evening,' I whispered.

I think his sudden appearance had given us all a start. We watched him totter away. Then Harry said, briskly, 'Now Aaron, we dare you to take away one of these stones.'

A passing car lit up Aaron's face for a second. He looked pretty sick, actually. But he just said, 'All right, if this is what you want me to do, if it means so much to you.' And there was no hiding the bitterness in his voice. For a moment I felt ashamed, as if we had no business forcing Aaron to do this. But the feeling quickly disappeared.

Aaron bent down, hesitated, then picked up this stone: one of the oddest-looking stones there, shaped like a bone.

Aaron stood staring down at the stone in his hand, as if he didn't know what it was. Then, from faraway came the sound of a dog

howling: high and mournful. At once, Aaron's hand started to shake violently, as if the stone was burning him. He let the stone fall out of his hand and on to the ground. But even after he'd let the stone drop, Aaron's hand was still shaking.

'I'm not messing about with this,' he cried. He sounded dead scared. Then he ran away from us and over towards his dad.

For a moment, we were too stunned to speak. Finally, Laura cried, 'We've done it.'

'It's just amazing,' said Harry, his face one big grin. 'He was so big-headed in the hut, saying all ghost stories were a load of rubbish . . . and then he comes out here and just flips.'

We all smiled at each other triumphantly.

'Did you see the way his hand was shaking when he picked up that stone?' exclaimed Laura.

'And he reckoned he was such a hard man,' I said. 'We've blown his cover all right, haven't we?'

'He's nothing really, is he?' said Harry. All three of us were laughing excitedly now.

'Hurry up you three,' cried Roy suddenly. He didn't sound any too happy. I wondered if he had guessed what we'd been up to.

'I think we should take a stone away,' said Laura.

'Good idea,' I replied. 'It'll be something to show our friend Aaron, won't it?'

Then we all hesitated: 'So who's going to pick the stone up then?' I asked.

Laura suddenly bent down and picked up the same stone Aaron had held a few minutes ago. 'There,' she gasped, 'I've done it.'

As she spoke, that dog howled again, louder and more mournfully than before, She laughed a little breathlessly. 'Come on, let's have some fun with this stone.'

CHAPTER FOUR

It was Laura's idea.

She would take the stone with her into Carrie's bedroom. Then, half an hour later, she would run on to the landing claiming she'd just seen the ghost dog. Harry and I would make a big fuss and see if we could get Aaron scared again.

With anyone else we would have stopped by now. But having discovered Aaron's weakness it was too exhilarating not to go on.

Harry was on a camp bed in my room, and kept whispering about tonight's events.

Every so often Harry would do an impression of a chicken and we'd both start giggling. Aaron ignored all our antics. He pretended he was asleep. But I knew he wasn't. I looked at my watch; any second now Laura would run out of her bedroom.

Just then I heard a bedroom door open and footsteps walking across the landing. I lay waiting for Laura to start crying out about the terrible ghost dog she'd seen. But nothing happened. I sat up in bed. 'Harry,' I whispered.

There was no answer. 'Harry, you're not asleep, are you?'

'No, I'm not asleep,' muttered Harry. But

he was speaking really slowly; he sounded as if he were talking at the wrong speed.

I lay back again and waited for Laura's signal . . . and waited.

'Harry,' I whispered. 'What do you think's happened to Laura?'

Harry just gave a snore in reply.

So it was up to me to find out. I climbed out of bed and went on to the landing, I saw Laura rightaway. She was standing under the landing light, which was always left on at night.

'Laura,' I whispered.

But she didn't turn around.

'Laura,' I called again, only this time much louder.

She gave a kind of jump, then whirled round, her eyes wide with terror.

I sprang forward. 'Laura, what is it? What's wrong?'

She didn't say anything, just started to shake.

I took hold of her hand. 'Laura, tell me what's happened?' She continued to shake. I was getting panicky now. 'Laura, speak to me.'

Instead, she just shook her head at me. It was then I remembered something.

The first time I'd met Laura was at infant school and she wouldn't speak to me. In fact, she wouldn't speak to anyone. Miss Bailey, our form teacher, said Laura was very sensitive and very shy and we mustn't force her to speak.

So, for some days Laura played with us and went to all our lessons without uttering one single word. It was very strange, especially as everyone else in the class talked non-stop.

In a way it made Laura quite intriguing.

Then one day Miss Bailey wanted volunteers to be in a play about different birds and animals. And when Miss Bailey asked who wanted to be the nightingale, Laura's hand shot up. Everyone was astonished. But Miss Bailey picked Laura to be the nightingale. Later, when we started reading the play aloud Laura spoke for the first time – as the nightingale. She's gone on speaking ever since – until tonight.

'Laura, can't you speak?' I whispered. Laura shook her head, getting more and more agitated.

'That's all right,' I said, gently. 'Not talking is fine. Let's go to the kitchen. I'll make you a milkshake if you like.' Laura's face briefly lit up. She can't resist milkshakes.

So with my arm around her we slowly walked down to the kitchen. Then I set about making Laura a strawberry milkshake. I thought my mum or Roy might hear me and come charging downstairs demanding to know what I was doing. But no-one did.

I gave Laura the milkshake which she gulped down. 'Another one?' I asked. She nodded eagerly. While Laura was drinking her second strawberry milkshake I said, 'Do you remember what you said when you played the nightingale?'

At once Laura replied, 'I may look brown and ordinary but when I sing I have the most beautiful voice in the world.' Then she stopped and said in a kind of wonderment, 'My voice has come back. I thought I'd lost it again, I really did.'

'What happened, Laura?' I said, gently.

She started to shiver. 'I saw it,' she gasped.

'Saw what?'

'The ghost dog,' she cried, and all at once she was talking really quickly. 'It was waiting for me. I fell asleep and there it was. I saw its evil red eyes staring at me. And I called out; "What do you want?" Then I heard it say, "You, I've come back for you," and as it spoke blood poured out of its mouth. It was the most horrible thing I'd ever seen in my life. And it was so close to me . . . I tried to scream.

'Only no sounds came out of my mouth. Instead, I jumped awake. But I could still sense the creature was somewhere near me.

So I ran to the landing and stood under the light. Sometimes if I think about ghosts at home I'll go and stand under the landing light for a while and that always helps me, then I can go back to sleep. But this time it didn't help. Instead I kept seeing pictures in the light... pictures of that terrible dog with blood dripping out of his mouth.' She started to shake again.

'Can you see it now?' I asked.

'No, no,' she said. 'I think it's gone at last.' She turned to her milkshake and slurped up the remains of it. Her voice fell. 'I feel a bit silly now.'

'Well, don't,' I replied. 'I mean, tonight has been quite eerie, what with going to that old churchyard.'

'And hearing that dog howl,' said Laura.
'Yeah, that was a bit strange,' I agreed. 'So
for a few minutes you forgot it wasn't real.
But remember, there's no such thing as the
ghost dog, actually.'

'Oh, I know,' said Laura.
'We just made it up, to scare Aaron.'
'And we did scare Aaron, didn't we?'
Laura smiled. 'The way he dropped that
stone as if it had just bitten him . . .' Then
she added, 'You won't tell anyone about
tonight, will you?'

'Of course not,' I replied. 'It's our secret for ever.'

'Thanks, Dan.'

'That's OK. After all, you never told about the time *The Wizard of Oz* scared me. Remember?'

'Oh, yes,' cried Laura. 'It was the trees you didn't like, wasn't it?'

'That's right. And the way they kept moving about and talking . . . that really gave me the creeps.' I shook my head. 'Imagine being scared by *The Wizard of Oz*, that's deeply shaming, but you never gave my secret away – so one good turn deserves another.'

We crept upstairs, whispering together. But when we reached Laura's room, she said, 'Wait there a moment, will you, Dan?' And when she returned she was holding the stone in her hand. 'Would you mind keeping this for the rest of the night, please?' she asked.

'No, sure. Of course not,' I said, as confidently as I could. Inside my bedroom Aaron and Harry were both snoring. I put the stone on my little cabinet then I climbed into bed.

'It's just a stone,' I kept saying to myself.

73

But still, it took me ages to get to sleep. I couldn't help thinking about that ghost dog too.

The next thing I knew Mum was drawing the curtains and asking us how we'd all slept. I blinked and smiled. Not even the whisper of a dream about the ghost dog. I felt ashamed of myself for even thinking such a thing.

'All right lads, rise and shine,' said Mum as she opened the bedroom window wide. 'That's what this room needs, fresh air . . . breakfast in ten minutes.'

At once, Aaron rushed off to the bathroom.

'He'll be in there for ages now,' I moaned to Harry.

But Harry just muttered: 'Why is everyone up so early?' and fell asleep again. In the end I left Harry sleeping while I got dressed.

As I came out of the bathroom I bumped into Laura. She looked very pale and tired. 'How are you?' I asked.

'I'm OK,' said Laura quietly. Then her voice rose. 'Don't tell anyone about last night, will you?'

'Of course not, I promised.'

'Not even Harry?'

'OK, not even Harry.'

She gave a faint smile. 'Thanks, Dan . . . I'm ashamed. That horrible dream seems so silly now.' She shivered. 'Yet last night . . .'

'You just got a bit carried away,' I interrupted. 'You do that sometimes. What about that play where you had to cry at the end, and then you couldn't stop crying?'

'Yes, I remember, I do get carried away.' That thought seemed to reassure her. 'And that's what happened to me last night.' Laura gave another half-smile.

My bedroom door burst open, and there was Harry standing in his pyjamas. His hair was all sticking up at the back and he was yawning and looked so sleepy that Laura and I both burst out laughing.

'I could sleep for another week,' he muttered. Then he grinned. 'It was a brilliant crack with Aaron last night, wasn't it? Especially the moment when he was so scared he dropped the stone.' He started to laugh and we joined in, Laura rather uneasily.

'Do you suppose we gave Aaron any nightmares?' asked Harry. Laura half-turned away; a deep red blush was creeping up her neck.

'I'm sure we did,' I replied.

Harry gave another triumphant grin before falling into the bathroom.

After breakfast I went into town with Laura and Harry. We hung around the sports shop where we met up with mates from school. Then we went ice-skating. By the evening, though, I was dead tired, so I just crashed out on the sofa watching some videos Roy had bought. Suddenly, from upstairs we heard, 'Mummy, can I have a drink please?'

'Oh, Carrie, I thought you were asleep hours ago,' cried Mum. 'All right, I won't be a minute.'

As Mum left, Roy said, 'OK boys, bed-time for you two, I think.'

I didn't know if I liked Roy giving me orders. That was Mum's job, not his. Still, Aaron and I trooped upstairs in silence; we'd hardly spoken to each other all day. Aaron charged into the bathroom. It was good to have my bedroom to myself for a few minutes.

I picked up the stone from last night. I was going to put it in the box by my wardrobe where I kept all my junk. But I took one last look at it. It fascinated me. It was so jagged and heavy; it was a bit like one of those axes cavemen used. Maybe it had been. Stones can be thousands of years old. I was just thinking about this when I heard a loud sighing behind me.

Aaron was glaring at me.

'What's the matter with you?' I asked.

Aaron shook his head. 'You're pathetic.'

'What are you going on about?' I demanded.

'You and that stone, you think you're so funny, don't you.'

'I was just looking at it,' I began.

'Yeah, yeah, I know what you were doing. That stone, you couldn't just have got rid of it like any normal person, could you? No, you've got to keep it here.'

'What's it to you, anyway?' I said. 'Unless this stone scares you.'

'Oh yeah, I mean, it's such a scary stone, isn't it?' jeered Aaron.

'Well, you were afraid to take it home,' I taunted.

'No, I wasn't.'

'Yes, you were,' I cried. 'Your hand was shaking when you held that stone.'

'Yeah, it was shaking with laughter.'

'You liar,' I cried.

Aaron's voice began to rise. 'Do you think I believed that stupid story you told me?'

'You believed every word and you dropped that stone because you were scared out of your wits.'

'I was not.' Aaron was practically screaming at me now.

'Scared out of your wits,' I repeated.

My bedroom door flew open and Mum and Roy were standing there.

'We were just discussing something,' I mumbled.

'Well, you were making far too much noise,' began Mum. Then all at once Roy exploded beside her. 'I don't know what's going on in here. You've got this nice big room with plenty of space for two people. So what's the big problem . . . WHAT IS THE PROBLEM?' Roy stopped for breath. His mouth had gone down at the corners and his eyes were bulging: at me. Roy had obviously decided I was the main culprit here.

'I think you both behaved badly,' cut in Mum, perhaps to stop Roy going on with his very biased view of events, 'and I think the sooner you both get to sleep the better.' She half-pushed Roy out of the bedroom. He looked as if he had a bit more to say: all against me, no doubt.

I lay in my bunk, stunned. I'd quite liked Roy before. But tonight, he'd shown himself in his true colours. Whatever happened, it would always be me in the wrong, never his precious son.

I glared down at Aaron. 'Been crying to your daddy about me, haven't you?'

'I wouldn't waste a second talking about you,' snapped Aaron.

I was shaking with anger now. I didn't want Aaron in my house, in my bedroom. He was just ruining everything. In the end I was shaking so much I had to get up. I let Rocky out. He kept on wanting to be stroked, so I just sat on the floor, stroking him and whispering, 'One day we'll have this room to ourselves again.' After a while I began to feel sleepy so I put Rocky in his cage and got back into bed again.

It still took me ages to get off to sleep, though. I was tossing and turning until finally I was walking somewhere. There was a heavy, grey mist so I couldn't see where I was going. I just knew the ground felt soft and squelchy: as if it were trying to drag me down into it. And the air was so cold and stale it was making me cough.

Where was I? I didn't like this place. I wanted to be away from here. And then I caught a glimpse of something, the tree which was bent double. Here it was, looking more sad and pathetic than ever. And beside it were all the stones. The stones which were supposed to mark the dog's grave.

I must be back in the old churchyard. Only I couldn't make out anything else. I coughed again. The mist seemed to be getting into my lungs.

Then from out of nowhere came this howling noise. The same howling we'd heard that night at the churchyard. Only this time it sounded much louder. I peered around. I was being watched. Just a few feet away from me were a pair of eyes: bright, burning red eyes that looked right through me. I could feel my heart beating in my mouth, I was too terrified to move. At first.

Suddenly, I was running, as fast as I could. But it was very hard to run on this soft mud. It was like trying to run in quicksand. And then I sensed hot breath on my neck. It was right behind me. It'll get me, I must run faster ... faster ... I jumped awake, gasping for breath, and my heart was still pounding furiously.

'Calm down. It's over,' I told myself. Through the curtains I could see a faint, grey light. It was still very early. I should go back to sleep. But I daren't. For I knew what would be waiting for me.

So instead, I just lay there hour after hour, envying Aaron his calm, restful sleep. I heard the clatter and jangle of the paper boy slamming the Sunday papers through the letterbox, and then the phone started to ring, loudly, urgently.

My mum had a phone in her room, so I heard her say, in a very sleepy voice, '784612.' And then: 'Well, I'll see if he's awake. It is Sunday morning, you know.' Then Mum appeared in my doorway. 'Dan, are you awake?'

'Yes, I'm awake,' I said. I'd been awake half the night.

'It's Laura on the phone for you. She sounds quite upset. Do you want to take it in the kitchen?'

I shot downstairs to the kitchen.

'Hi, Laura.'

'I didn't wake you up, did I?'

'No, not at all. What's up?'

She was speaking very slowly: 'Dan, it came back last night. That ghost dog. I saw it, and it scared me so much.' There was a pause before she whispered, 'Dan, what am I going to do?'

'Don't worry,' I said. 'I saw it last night too.'

'You did,' she exclaimed.

'So you're not the only one,' I said. 'And listen, we're going to sort this out. I'll be round your house rightaway.'

CHAPTER FIVE

Laura was waiting outside her house for me.

'I came as fast as I could,' I gasped. And although we don't normally do anything corny, I gave her hand a squeeze.

Her mum welcomed me enthusiastically. 'Come to cheer Laura up, have you? Splendid. She had a bad nightmare last night. Tea and toast for both of you?' We both nodded eagerly.

Laura whispered, 'Mum just thinks I had a nightmare. She's been really nice to me. So's Dad. She doesn't know anything about the ghost dog.'

Over tea and toast we compared our nightmares. They were pretty similar. Only Laura was in a wood when she saw the ghost dog, not in the churchyard.

'I think it would be even worse seeing it in that old churchyard,' said Laura.

'It was,' I agreed. 'All the ground was soggy and you could hardly run in it . . . still, it must have been pretty scary in the wood.'

'I kept running into the branches of trees,' said Laura, 'and twice I fell over. When I woke up I really thought I'd sprained my ankle, just like you did at your party.'

Laura's mum appeared again. 'Phone for you, Laura,' she said.

Laura rushed off and was gone some time. When she came back, she said, 'You'll never guess who that was?'

'Father Christmas.'

'No, Harry.'

'I was close, then. So what did old Harry want?'

'He says he saw it too . . . the ghost dog.'

I gazed at her, stunned. 'Are you sure he wasn't messing about?'

Laura shook her head. 'He sounded really worked up. He said he'd tried ringing you but your mum told him you were here. He's coming over too.'

And a few minutes later there was a sur- prisingly serious Harry, also having tea and toast. He had seen the ghost dog outside his house. It was getting dark and he was about to draw the curtains when he heard a terri- ble howling noise. And then he saw this huge dog banging its head against the glass, struggling to get in. He was absolutely terri- fied and woke himself up, yelling loudly.

I shook my head in astonishment. So the ghost dog had appeared in all three of our dreams last night. 'Well, you certainly can't say this dog is lazy. He keeps busy, doesn't he?' I said.

Laura and Harry managed small smiles. 'How long do you think this will go on?' asked Harry. 'Will he turn up again tonight?'

'I don't think so,' I said. 'I'm sure it's over now. I mean, look, what we've got to remember is, the ghost dog isn't real. I made it all up.'

'Are you sure?' asked Harry, suddenly. 'Where did that story about the dog and his grave come from?'

I shrugged my shoulders. 'My imagination.'

'But you thought you saw something when you switched the hall light off to play *Murder in the Dark*,' said Laura.

'A dog, wasn't it?' murmured Harry.

All of a sudden they were both staring intently at me.

'All right,' I said. 'I might have seen something then, although that was probably just imagination too. And everything else

90

certainly was. There's no such thing as the ghost dog.'

Harry and Laura looked at me doubtfully. Then Harry said, quietly, 'I think we should take the stone back.'

'Why?' I exclaimed.

'The dog said, if anyone took so much as one stone away from his grave he would haunt them for ever,' said Harry, in the same quiet tone.

'Now you're being really stupid,' I cried. 'We made that curse up. In fact, you made that part up, Harry.'

'Did I?' Harry sounded puzzled.

'Yes, don't you remember Aaron said my story was a load of old rubbish, so to try and scare him you added the bit about the stone.'

'But it wouldn't do any harm to take the stone back,' began Laura.

'Yes, it would,' I interrupted. 'That stone is nothing. I'd feel really stupid taking it back. It would be like we'd ended up fooling ourselves.'

'Look, Dan,' said Harry. 'That dream really freaked me out last night. And I don't want to see that ghost dog again. He's too noisy for a start, howling and head-banging. All the neighbours are complaining . . .' Then he added, almost pleadingly, 'If you don't want to go, give the stone to Laura and me. We'll take it back.'

'That stone is staying in my bedroom,' I said. 'You and Laura are just being daft.'

Laura's mum appeared to clear away. 'More tea, anyone?'

'We couldn't eat another thing,' I replied.

Laura's mum smiled, then she said, 'Laura's lucky to have friends like you, rushing round to cheer her up. Nightmares can be so powerful, can't they? Poor Laura couldn't stop shaking when she woke up.'

I looked across at Laura's pale face. Her eyes looked very large this morning. I couldn't help feeling a stab of sympathy for her. And although all three of us had made the story up, I'd started it, hadn't I? I was the most to blame.

So after Laura's mum had gone, I said, 'OK, if you really want to take the stone back, we will.'

'Dan, put it there,' said Harry, shaking my hand.

'Can we do it today?' asked Laura.

So after lunch I went up to my room and took the stone out of my wardrobe. As I stared at it I thought I could make out bits of faces: a nose here, an eye there. 'This stone's certainly got charisma,' I said to myself. But to be honest, I wasn't altogether sorry to be getting rid of it.

It was a damp, drizzly afternoon when the three of us set off. By the time we reached the churchyard it was already quite dark. But then this seemed the kind of place where it was always grey and gloomy. We found the old bent tree easily. It looked exactly as it

had in my nightmare. My heart started to thump.

The clock in the church tower chimed loudly above us. We all stared at the church for a moment.

'They say you can see shapes in the church windows,' said Laura. 'They're supposed to be angels watching us.'

'Well, we need all the help we can get,' I said briskly.

'Maybe the angels are cross with us,' said Laura.

'What are you rabbiting on about?' I asked.

'Well, we were a bit nasty to Aaron last night, weren't we?' said Laura. 'Me, included,' she added hastily.

'*We* were nasty!' I exclaimed. 'What about him, sneering at us and . . . ?'

'Oh, I know he deserved it,' interrupted Laura.

'And how would you like to have Aaron in your bedroom every night?' I ranted on.

'I don't think he'd be allowed in Laura's bedroom every night,' said Harry, trying to make a joke of it all. 'And look, can we just get this over with?'

'OK then,' I said, taking the stone from my pocket.

'Do you think we ought to say something?' asked Laura.

'What do you suggest? Goodbye, Mr Stone, have a nice life?' I replied.

'There's no need to be sarky,' she said, quietly. 'I just think we should say we're sorry for disturbing it.'

'Well, you can say that, I'm not,' I said, handing her the stone.

It was exactly then a dog started to bark. I must admit it gave us all a start and Laura nearly dropped the stone with shock. 'Dogs are always barking, aren't they?' she gasped.

'That's right, it's just here we notice it more,' I said.

The rain was starting to come down really heavily now and it was becoming colder, too. That probably explains why we'd all started shivering.

'We're so sorry for disturbing you,' said Laura, in a voice so low I could hardly hear her. 'We should never have done it. But we've brought you back, so please leave us in peace now.'

'I've heard it all now,' I muttered, 'grovelling to a stone.'

Laura continued to look serious as she very gently lowered the stone on to the ground. Part of me wanted to laugh. But another part of me felt uneasy. I really didn't like this place. I gave a kind of half-shiver, then said, 'It's funny, really, we invent this story about the stone, and the ghost dog, to scare Aaron and he's the only one who's not here, getting soaked to the skin.'

Harry gave a small smile. 'That trick back-fired on us, all right. Still, it's all over now, so come on, let's get out of here.'

We walked quickly away, practically sprinting up Church Walk. It was only when we were back in the village High Street that we started to slow down. 'I've just remembered,' I cried. 'We've got to go back. I've forgotten something.'

'What?' cried Laura.

'I was going to take another stone away, just as a souvenir.'

'Yeah, yeah, yeah,' grinned Harry. 'We do believe you.' And then all three of us were laughing with relief. 'I'll tell you something for nothing,' said Harry. 'I never want to go back to that place again.'

'I wouldn't go if you paid me,' declared Laura.

'Well, I might, if you paid me,' I said. But then I added, 'No, I never want to go back there again either.'

'So where shall we go?' asked Harry.

'How about walking into town? McDonald's will be open,' said Laura.

Inside McDonald's we all pigged out on Big Macs, chips and chocolate milkshakes. Then Harry ordered some chicken nuggets.

'You're hungry,' said Laura.

'Not really,' replied Harry. 'Just very relieved.'

I knew exactly what he meant.

When I got home, Mum was waiting for me.

'Can I have a quick word?'

'You can have a long word, if you like,' I said.

'It's about Aaron,' began Mum. Inside I groaned. I should have guessed. 'Roy's going away in a few minutes,' she went on, 'and I think Aaron's quite upset about that. He's hardly eaten a thing all day.'

'Oh, no, what a tragedy,' I said, with undisguised sarcasm.

'Now, don't be like that,' said Mum. 'You can be such a thoughtful boy when you like. Be helpful to Aaron . . . for my sake, please.'

Just then Roy and Aaron appeared. Roy was all smiles, patting me on the head and even giving me a small present. But his cover had been blown. I knew that he'd always see everything just from Aaron's point of view.

Roy gave Mum a hug goodbye, and I heard him whispering to her, 'Look, we really can work this out, you know.' I wondered what he meant by that, and hoped it wasn't anything to do with me. I bet it was. Then Roy gave Aaron a punch and told him to 'get involved', shook hands with me, and kissed the top of Carrie's head.

'That tickled,' she muttered.

Later, Mum was saying to Aaron, 'He'll be back before you know it. The weeks will just fly by.' Aaron didn't really reply and his face was expressionless, dead. It was hard to know if he was upset or not.

I went to my bedroom quite early that night. Aaron was already there, lying in his bunk reading a book. Neither of us spoke. There was a tense, uncomfortable silence. Once or twice I did try and say something, just to break the awful atmosphere. But everything I thought of sounded silly and I didn't want to say anything which Aaron could sneer at. So in the end I just chatted to Rocky.

Then I clambered up into bed. I nearly called out, 'Night,' but lost my nerve. Instead, I tried to get to sleep. I expected to lie awake for hours, but instead I fell asleep almost at once, and found myself in a place where it was dark and misty, and wet. Even before I saw the old bent tree, I knew where I was.

The mist had thickened tonight wrapping itself around everything, except . . . Nothing could hold this creature back. There it was, looming over me: bigger than ever. Only tonight, its massive jaws were half-open. I always hate it when you can see a dog's sharp teeth. Now I could make out something else. Blood dripping from its mouth. The blood of one of its other victims. Like Laura or Harry. And once it had got the taste for humans . . .

Suddenly, it lunged forward and I let out such a terrible scream I woke myself up. Waves of sweat were rolling off me. I pushed the covers off. I still felt as if I were burning up, while shivers were running up and down my back.

It was so close tonight. If I hadn't woken up then, that dog would have got me for sure. Maybe it had got Laura or Harry. Should I ring and find out? No, their parents would go mad.

100

What I didn't understand was: we'd taken the stone back. The dog should leave us alone now. But then I remembered the original curse: the dog said, if anyone took so much as one stone away from his grave he would haunt them for ever. There was nothing about what the dog would do if you took the stone back.

Maybe, once we'd released the dog into our dreams, that was it. There was no letting go of it after that. Every night now for the rest of our lives Laura, Harry and I would see that dog, until . . . another part of the story flashed into my head. The dog went on haunting the boy until the boy was found dead with a look of such terror on his face . . . After that I had to get out of bed and start pacing around my room. Why had I made up such a stupid story? For now the story was in our heads and we couldn't get rid of it. The dog could be attacking Laura or Harry now.

And it was mostly my fault.

I climbed back into bed. Below me Aaron was fast asleep, but making those funny breathing noises. I drifted off to sleep but I kept thinking I saw the ghost dog and jumping awake.

At breakfast time I staggered downstairs. I gave Rocky some Marmite on toast which he gobbled down. But I wasn't at all hungry and neither, strangely enough, was Aaron. Mum tut-tutted in annoyance. 'Breakfast is the most important meal of the day, you know. What's the matter with you both?'

'Just not hungry, Mum,' I said weakly. Outside, Harry and Laura were waiting for me. I was actually relieved to see them. I'd had this horrible vision of them being so badly mauled by the dog that they couldn't escape and had to stay in that nightmare. But as soon as I saw their pale, tense faces, I knew they'd been visited by the ghost dog too.

'I was in the wood and this thing jumped out of the bushes at me,' cried Laura.

'It nearly got in the house,' said Harry. 'I saw this dark shadow scraping at the door so hard. Next time . . .'

'What are we going to do?' cried Laura. She and Harry were looking at me expectantly.

And right then it came to me. Yes, of course, why hadn't I thought of that before?

'I've got an idea,' I said.

CHAPTER SIX

That evening Harry, Laura and me went back to the hut. It was my idea.

'So, come on,' said Harry to me, 'you can tell us now. Why have you got us to come back here?'

I leaned forward. 'This is the place where we created the ghost dog . . .'

'So,' interrupted Harry.

'So, this seems the ideal place to tame it.'

'Tame it?' echoed Laura.

'That's right,' I said. 'Tonight we're going to tame the ghost dog by telling funny stories about it. Then the next time we see it we'll just burst out laughing and it won't be able to scare us any more.' Laura and Harry looked at me doubtfully. 'Look,' I exclaimed, 'we made the dog spooky, so we can make it . . .' I searched for the right word, 'unspooky.' Laura and Harry looked at me doubtfully. I pressed on. 'First of all we need to give it a stupid name, like, The Mutt.'

'Or Goofy,' cried Laura.

'Or what about Spurs,' said Harry. 'That's a really stupid name, especially for a football team.' Both he and Laura were Manchester United supporters.

'Here, watch it,' I said, 'or we'll be calling it Man United, for sure.'

'How about Bonzo or Gonzo,' said Laura.

'Gonzo,' I repeated. 'That's a really silly name for a dog. Come on, Gonzo, walkies.' I started to laugh. 'So tonight when you see the dog, or if you do,' I added hastily, seeing Laura's anxious face, 'call out, Gonzo, here Gonzo.'

'And you can keep calling out Gonzo as it pulls your leg off,' said Harry.

'Oh come on, give this a chance,' I replied. 'Now, what else would make this dog look really silly?'

'A pink ribbon,' suggested Laura.

'Brilliant,' I cried. 'I can see it now, Gonzo in a pink ribbon.'

'And one of those silly dog coats as well,' said Laura.

'Why not?' I agreed. 'This dog is going to look so daft tonight.'

'How about if it's wearing glasses?' asked Harry.

'I don't know,' said Laura. 'That might make his red eyes even bigger.'

'Tinted glasses, then,' suggested Harry.

'I think we should leave the glasses, but it should definitely have one of those high-pitched barks,' I said.

'And whenever you hum it starts dancing,' cried Laura.

'Now that would be a real crack,' I laughed.

'But tonight, will it . . .?' began Laura, doubtfully.

'Gonzo will do all of these daft things because it's our dog. We made it. But we've got to keep seeing Gonzo doing things like that.'

At once all three of us started concentrating hard on Gonzo with his pink ribbon and dog coat, and dancing away to any tune we hummed.

'When I see that dog tonight,' said Harry, 'I'm just going to laugh and laugh and laugh.'

'What will happen to Gonzo when we laugh at it?' asked Laura.

'He will get smaller,' I replied, 'until finally he will shrink away to nothing.'

'I've got this picture in my head now,' said Laura, 'of first of all its body disappearing, then its legs, and finally there's just this head floating around, until that starts to fade away too.'

'I don't care how it disappears,' said Harry, 'just provided it does – and it never comes back again either.'

'Well, if it does try to return we just laugh at it again, then it will soon go. And remember, call out Gonzo when you see it,' I said.

'Gonzo,' Harry grinned. 'You could almost feel sorry for a dog with a name like that. Almost.'

We left the hut in an optimistic, cheerful mood. But back in my house, I just felt scared again. What if my idea didn't work?

'Time for bed,' called Mum.

'OK,' I replied. But I didn't move. The phone rang. It was Laura. 'I'm just ringing up for a chat and a bit of confidence,' she whispered.

Talking to Laura made me feel certain again. My plan would work.

Mum appeared. I thought she was going to tell me off for not being in bed. Instead, she asked, 'Did you have a good time?' She was smiling, sort of.

'Yeah, great.'

'Were you telling ghost stories again?' she asked.

'Something like that. Only funnier ones.'

'Aaron's still not eating properly,' she said, suddenly. 'But every time I say anything he tells me he's just not hungry.' Now Mum was looking to me for a bit of confidence. She did that sometimes, especially when she was worried about Carrie.

'He's just missing Roy,' I said. 'When's Roy back from America, then?'

Mum's face grew even tenser. 'I really don't know,' she said. Then she added: 'If Aaron does try and talk to you, don't . . . well, give him a chance.'

'I'm the last person he'd talk to. He'd be more likely to talk to Carrie than me.'

Mum gave another sigh and disappeared. She seemed really wound up tonight.

Upstairs, Aaron was asleep already. After saying 'Goodnight' to Rocky I got into bed too. My eyes burned with tiredness. I closed them. I tried to picture Gonzo wearing a pink ribbon, a dog coat and glasses . . . no, not glasses. Not even tinted ones . . . When I opened my eyes again I saw it rightaway, crouched in the darkness.

I peered through the mist. Yes, it was

wearing a pink ribbon all right. And a dog coat.

My plan was working.

That made me a little more confident. 'Gonzo,' I whispered. 'Gonzo.'

All at once those red eyes were beamed right at me. Some of my confidence oozed away again. We should have changed the dog's eyes: made them smaller. I suppose it was too late now.

And then it gave this very low snarl.

'That's not how you bark, you've got a high-pitched bark,' I cried.

At once the dog started making this very shrill yelping sound. It sounded like someone playing the same high note over and over again. It set my teeth on edge. 'No, stop that.' The dog obeyed instantly. But then I heard it snarling again. I was becoming confused now. And scared.

I remembered this dog danced if you hummed a tune. Now that sight would make it look totally ridiculous. I hummed the first few bars of the theme tune to *Neighbours*. That was enough. The dog was on its feet. I gulped. It looked bigger than ever.

'Now, come on, dance,' I cried. The dog lumbered to its feet and made that low, snarling noise in its throat again.

'Dance,' I squeaked.

Instead the dog took a giant step towards me. My knees started knocking together and then I totally lost my bottle and ran for it. Only I didn't get very far. I ran straight into this tree and fell flat on my face. I lay there, floundering about in the mud, and sensed this shadow towering over me.

I slammed shut my eyes. At least I didn't have to see it. But I could still hear it breathing really heavily. I could smell its stale, rotting breath too. It must be very close to me. The smell was making me heave.

And then I felt sharp teeth cutting into my left leg. The pain was excruciating. 'NO, NO, NO, NO.'

I opened my eyes. But it was no good. I couldn't see anything but darkness now. What had happened to me? I was sick with fear until slowly it dawned on me, I had my hand clamped over my face.

I took my hand away and gazed around at my bedroom. I was back. But relief quickly turned to disappointment. I'd thought by making fun of the dog I could make it disappear. But it hadn't worked. Why? Because I was still scared of it, that's why. And the dog knew that. Now every night it would be waiting for me, and there would be no holding it back. It would . . .

It was then I heard a noise which made my whole body freeze. Something was scratching at the wall behind me. Something was trying to get in.

It was the ghost dog. It has followed me out of my dream. And now it was scratching its way into my bedroom – just like in the story I'd told. It had got a taste of my flesh and now it wants more.

I heard it again, louder this time: scratching wildly, fiercely. Nothing was going to stop it getting through. I wanted to bury my head under the sheets, pretend I hadn't heard anything, go to sleep. Only, I didn't dare do that because it would be waiting for me there, too.

So I didn't do anything. I couldn't. My whole body had gone numb. I just lay there, frozen to the spot until finally I thought, this must still be a dream, I haven't woken up. I rubbed my eyes. The scratching went on. Then I rubbed my eyes really hard. If anything, the noise became even louder.

So I must be awake, which means . . . which means, any second now that dog will come tearing into my bedroom. And tomorrow morning my mum will draw back the curtains and see me lying there, my face frozen for ever in a look of such terror she'll never be able to forget it.

I should try and escape, leg it downstairs. But what's the point? It'll find me there too. There's no escaping the ghost dog. I closed my eyes, then almost at once they flew open again. Someone was calling my name. 'Daniel, Daniel,' the voice called, loudly, urgently. There was a pause for a moment before the voice cried, 'Daniel, please help me.' It was then I realized who was calling me.

It was Aaron.

CHAPTER SEVEN

I climbed out of bed and switched on the light, and stood for a second under the bedroom light, just as Laura does when she's scared, and this helped to calm me down a bit.

That scratching noise had really got me worked up. Now, with the light on, it sounded fainter and less scary. Perhaps it was just a bird or something.

Then I went over to Aaron. 'Why have you been calling me?' I demanded. The only reply from Aaron was a heavy, rhythmic, breathing noise. He must have called my name out in his sleep. How strange.

Then I watched Aaron raise his right hand and start scratching the wall behind him. So it was he who'd been scaring me half to death. For a second I was relieved, then I was mad. Trust Aaron to be the cause of the scratching noise. But then he caused all the hassle in my life. It was Aaron's fault we made up that story about the ghost dog. He was to blame for everything. I didn't really believe that, but it was good to dump all the blame on to someone else.

I glared down at Aaron just as he opened his eyes. He stared up at me, totally bewildered. 'What do you want?'

'You called me,' I replied shortly.

'I did what?' he asked, in that superior tone of his, which I hated so much.

'Just forget it,' I snapped. 'But you woke me up calling my name and scratching at the wall.' Aaron noticed he still had his right hand raised. He hastily lowered it. 'But if you want to pretend you didn't call me, then that's fine.' I made as if to climb back into bed.

That's when Aaron said, 'Yes, I did call you.' He whispered this as if he were confessing to some terrible crime.

'Make your mind up, won't you,' I snapped. But I was more embarrassed than angry. I hovered awkwardly in front of him. 'Why did you call me?' And my voice came out like a croak. It felt very strange talking to Aaron.

Aaron didn't reply at first. Then when he did speak he swallowed his words as if he couldn't hold them in his mouth very easily. 'I guess I needed your help.'

'You needed my help,' I repeated incredulously.

'I've needed your help for some days, actually, but I didn't tell you before because . . .' He shrugged his shoulders. 'But what does that matter now?' He half-looked at me. 'All right, you win.'

I shook my head. 'I don't understand.'

Aaron's voice started to rise. 'The dog you told me about to try and scare me, well you succeeded all right. Every night I see it and it terrifies the life out of me all right.' He was clenching his hands into fists as he went on.

'That dog, that monster has really got to me. I can't stop thinking about it. Even during the day it's like this giant shadow . . . I've even lost my appetite, which I thought would never happen.' He clenched his fists even tighter and stared down at them. 'So, like I said, you win, OK.'

'Where do you see this dog?' I asked.

'Same place every night, in the old churchyard that we went to.'

I started. So he'd seen the ghost dog in exactly the same place as I had.

'Tonight,' said Aaron, 'the dog had this pink ribbon on and he was wearing a kind of coat.'

120

That stunned me.

'But somehow,' went on Aaron, 'that just made it more weird and scary.'

'The story about the dog,' I said, slowly, 'it's not really true. I made it up to scare you.'

'Oh I guessed that,' replied Aaron at once. 'Still, I've got to admit, it scared me all right.'

I edged closer to Aaron: 'We scared ourselves too,' I admitted. 'Harry and Laura see the dog every night.' I stared down at his blue bed cover. 'And so do I.'

'You see it,' he gasped.

'Lucky me, huh,' I smiled grimly. Then staring even more intently at the blue bed cover, I said, 'Since you moved in here it's all been a bit of a disaster, hasn't it?'

'A total disaster,' agreed Aaron. 'But I know I did it all wrong. You see, I didn't want to move away from my old school, I had some brilliant mates there. But since my mum died, we're always on the move. Dad says he's got itchy feet and now he's jetting off to America. But I want to . . . I hate all this moving about.'

Then speaking all in a rush, he went on, 'That Spiderman costume, I should never

121

have worn that to your party. It was far too flash. But Dad would have been offended if I hadn't and he sulks, you know. Wouldn't speak to me for three days once. So I was stuck. Still, I can't blame people for hating me that night. Although most of them hated me long before that . . .' His voice rose. 'You turned everyone against me, didn't you?'

I could feel myself turning bright red. 'I thought you were trying to steal my friends,' I muttered. Yet, even as I said them, the words sounded so feeble and little kiddish: the sort of thing Carrie might say.

'I wasn't trying to steal your friends,' said Aaron.

'I know,' I replied.

'But I don't blame you,' went on Aaron. 'You've got to protect yourself. That's what we were both doing.'

Suddenly I stopped examining the bed cover and looked straight at Aaron. And he looked straight at me.

'Yeah, you've got to protect yourself,' I repeated quickly. 'But I'm sorry about . . . things.'

Aaron seemed slightly taken aback by this apology. And he let my sentence hang in the air for a moment. Finally, he asked, 'Do you think you can get rid of this dog?' He gave a confiding smile. 'I'm getting a bit desperate here.'

'I made the dog, so I should be able to get rid of it. Only, somehow I always end up running away from it.'

'I can see why,' said Aaron.

I shook my head. 'No, I shouldn't be running away from a dog I made up. That would be like an author being scared of one of his characters. Why, an author can just wipe out a character any time he likes. And so, that means . . . that means I can do it, too. Just wipe the dog out.' And as I said these words I could feel this tremendous power building up inside me. I'd had the same feeling when I made up the story of the ghost dog.

'Up to now,' I said, 'I've been really half-hearted and weedy, running away from the dog every time it so much as growled. But not any more . . . this time I'm going right up to it and face it and . . . well, it's up to me, isn't it.' And as I said these words I felt quite brave and heroic as if I were riding into battle to save others. 'Now, what's the time?'

'Just gone four,' said Aaron.

'Right, well there's still time to meet my monster, eyeball to eyeball.'

Aaron stared at me, grinning: 'What can I say, but good luck . . . and you're a mighty warrior.'

I grinned back. 'I'll probably lose all my courage before I go to sleep,' I said.

'No, you won't, Dan,' said Aaron, firmly. 'By the way, I probably won't go to sleep straightaway, so is it all right if I play with Rocky for a while?'

I felt a flash of irritation. Rocky was my pet, not his. But then I thought: where's the

harm in sharing Rocky? 'Yeah, sure, Rocky likes company,' I said. I closed my eyes; straightaway I could hear Aaron whispering to Rocky. I lay listening for a while and then I was faraway from them . . . faraway.

It felt different there this time. Perhaps because the wind was blowing really fiercely and the trees were shaking and sighing to themselves. It was as if they knew something was about to happen.

My heart began to beat furiously. This time, I couldn't fail.

'Gonzo, where are you?' I called. And then I saw it, just a few feet away from me. Or rather I saw those red eyes. The rest of it was, as usual, partly camouflaged by the thick grey mist.

Then, all at once the dog let out the most terrible howl I'd ever heard. Once that would have been enough to make me run for my life. And I'll admit, my legs wobbled more than a bit. But I told myself, I made this dog, I had the power.

I edged forward. The dog's eyes never left me. But I kept moving nearer to it. I'd told Aaron I'd face this dog eyeball to eyeball and that was what I was going to do.

Finally, I was just inches away from the dog. It was still wearing that pink ribbon and dog coat. But they just looked like a cheap joke now.

'That ribbon and coat should disappear,' I said. And to my total amazement, they did. They vanished rightaway.

Then I heard a voice say, 'Thank you, at least, for that, now go away before I bite you.'

The dog's voice was low and weary, like a very tired old man.

'I'm not going away. And you won't bite me,' I said.

As if in reply, the dog bared his teeth. I almost cried out, but nothing could stop me moving forward now. Suddenly my legs were as light as air. I wasn't so much walking as gliding.

And the nearer I got to those glowing, red eyes, the smaller they seemed.

Finally, I was right in front of the ghost dog. We were eyeball to eyeball as I'd promised Aaron. It was then the wind gave a deafening shriek and the mist started to shake as if it were being pulled away. And

that's exactly what happened. The mist flew right into my face and then was swept away.

For the first time the ghost dog wasn't camouflaged by the mist. I could see it really clearly.

And what I saw made me cry out with horror.

For the dog was nothing but skin and bone. I could even make out its rib cage. And it had little lumps all over its body: they were bruises, some of which were still bleeding.

'Who did this to you?' I cried

'Humans, who else?' said the dog. 'If my owner was feeling angry about something he'd throw me against the wall, made him feel better somehow.'

I started to shiver. This poor dog was in a terrible state. Why hadn't I noticed it before?

The least I could do was bathe the dog's wounds. But I needed a bowl of water and a sponge for that. I pictured them in my head and, rightaway, there was a bowl of water and a sponge beside me. 'I'm going to bathe your wounds,' I said.

The dog made as if to resist and tried to get to its feet, but it couldn't. It fell back to the ground again.

'You can hardly move,' I said. 'Yet, every night you chased after me.'

The dog shook its head. 'All I can do are a few tricks like this,' and it lifted back its head and gave this chilling howl which, even now, started my heart beating furiously. 'I'm pretty good at snarling too and showing my teeth. I leave the rest to your imagination.'

I felt rather foolish now. 'So each night I've been running away from nothing. We all have.'

The dog nodded. 'And very funny you looked too, running round and round in a circle every night.'

'What about the time I saw you at my

Halloween party, was that just imagination too?'

'Just imagination,' repeated the dog. 'Don't you know, nothing's stronger than imagination. Nothing.'

'But why did you let us go on scaring ourselves?'

'You have to protect yourself,' replied the dog.

'That's just what Aaron said,' I murmured, but I don't think the dog heard me, for it went on, 'Human beings have caused me so much pain, you know. How was I to know you were any different?'

'Let me at least bathe your wounds now,' I said, gently.

'You're wasting your time,' said the dog, but it didn't try and stop me.

'You must be in terrible pain,' I said.

The dog didn't answer this either, it just said, 'By the way, my name's not Gonzo, thank goodness.' It shuddered. 'It's Billy.'

'Billy, that's a good name,' I said.

'I know,' replied the dog, proudly.

When I'd finished I said, 'I expect you're hungry.'

'Not any more,' said the dog. 'I stopped
being hungry a long time ago. All I want is
for someone to make me a grave.'

I gave a little shiver. 'If that's what you
want I'll do that,' I said. 'But first you must
have something to eat.'

I pictured a bowl of mincemeat and then
saw it land in front of me. But Billy couldn't
get his head into the bowl very well, so I had
to feed him by hand. By the end he seemed
a lot better though, and I even conjured up
some dog biscuits for 'afters'.

'Now, do you still want me to make your
grave?' I asked.

'Yes, of course,' replied Billy. 'Then you'll know for certain I'll never bother you or your friends again. So follow me, as I've no wish to be buried here.'

Billy struggled to his feet and limped away. I followed him, trying to adjust to his very slow pace. And Billy led me into this wood. It was full of green trees and little clusters of flowers. And the sun was beaming down on us. I felt as if I'd wandered into a spring day.

'Where did this wood come from?' I exclaimed.

'Oh, it's always been here,' said Billy, casually. But he wagged his tail at me as if sharing my pleasure in this beautiful place. Then he became sad and serious again. 'I'd like to be buried right here,' he said.

'All right,' I replied and rightaway I started to dig. It took much longer than I'd expected, and when I'd finished sweat was pouring off me.

'How's that?' I gasped. 'That's deep enough, isn't it?'

Billy staggered to the edge of the grave and peered down. Then he looked up at me.

'I never thought a human would do that for me.'

I smiled at Billy and patted him on the head. At once his tail started to wag again, only this time his tail was wagging so fast I feared he might fall over. I bent down and started rubbing his chest. He really liked that.

Finally, Billy looked up at me and said: 'I've wanted a grave for so long but now – I don't want to go.'

'And I don't want you to go,' I cried, holding on to him really tightly.

But the next thing I knew Mum was calling, 'It's half-past seven,' and Billy had disappeared.

CHAPTER EIGHT

'All right, everyone,' called Harry. 'Shut up a minute and raise your can of Coke to Dan for getting rid of the ghost dog. Two whole weeks have gone by and not one nightmare between us. Cheers, Dan.' Cans of Coke were clinked and I tried to look pleased.

We were in the hut: the place where it had all started, celebrating the fact that it was all over.

'Of course the ghost dog was Dan's fault. He called it up,' grinned Harry, 'trying to frighten poor old Aaron.'

135

'I seem to remember I wasn't the only one trying to scare Aaron,' I said.

'Ah, but we're easily led,' replied Harry, his grin getting broader. He turned to Aaron. 'He made us do it, you know.'

'You all scared me something rotten,' said Aaron. 'And I can't tell you how good it is to sleep at night now. That's when I don't hear Dan whistling for Billy.'

I blushed. 'If you'd seen that dog and how badly it had been treated . . . and . . .'

'We know,' interrupted Harry. 'You told us once or twice,' and he gave a mock yawn. 'To be honest with you, Dan, I'm glad you can't find that dog. I'm really sorry for it but I don't want it popping up in any more of my dreams.'

'Or mine,' murmured Aaron.

Just then, there was a knock at the door.

'It's the ghost dog,' joked Harry.

Instead, my mum walked in, smiling nervously. 'I'm sorry to break up the fun, but I do need to have a word with Aaron and Daniel tonight.'

'Come on, what have they done?' cried Harry.

'Nothing,' I said, indignantly, before adding, 'Have we?'

'No, it's not a telling off,' said Mum.

'Shame,' muttered Harry.

Mum returned to the house, closely followed by Aaron and Harry. Laura waited for me.

'You're very quiet,' I said to her.

'Mmm.'

'What's up?'

'I've just been thinking,' she sighed, 'about the ghost dog . . . Billy. Maybe it's for the best. He wasn't very happy here, was he?'

'He was happy with me.'

'But you gave him what he wanted,' said Laura. 'You made him a grave.'

'Yeah, but . . . every night I'm in that churchyard, you know, whistling and calling for him. I know he's probably gone, but I'd really like to find him.'

Laura didn't answer. She just gave my hand a squeeze.

Inside the house Aaron was waiting for me. 'What do you reckon this is about?' he asked.

'I don't know. It doesn't feel like one of Mum's lectures, but you never know.'

'I bet she's heard from Dad,' said Aaron.

Mum was in the lounge. 'Have you heard from Dad at all?' asked Aaron cheerily.

'Yes, I have. He'll be here tomorrow night,' said Mum.

'Great. I haven't seen him for ages,' began Aaron. Then he stopped. Mum was looking really upset about something.

'What's wrong?' I asked.

'The thing is,' said Mum, slowly, 'Roy and I have decided to part. It hasn't been working out, so we both decided it would be for the best for all of us.' She paused. Aaron and I were too stunned to know what to say. 'So Roy will be arriving tomorrow evening to collect Aaron.' I just hated the way Mum said 'collect Aaron'. She made it sound as if Roy were popping round to pick up a parcel – not a person.

'Can't I stay a bit longer, until the end of term anyway?' asked Aaron.

'Roy wants to make a clean break,' said Mum in that same slow tone. 'He's picked out a school in America – a really good school – and they're happy to take you rightaway, so you can have Christmas in your new home.'

I shook my head in amazement. 'I can't believe this.'

'We will try and make sure you and Aaron still see each other,' said Mum.

'I reckon we will,' I cried, 'with Aaron in America and me here.'

'It won't be easy,' agreed Mum. 'But we'll arrange something. Roy and I will still be friends, of course . . .'

'Just like you and Dad are,' I snapped. Straightaway I wished I hadn't said that. Especially as Mum looked as if she was about to burst into tears. But I was angry and upset and I had to hit out at someone.

Actually, I think Mum knew that, because she said, quietly, 'I'll miss Aaron too, you know.'

Aaron and I sat up talking most of the night. We decided to tell Roy that Aaron didn't want to move away from here, and that was that.

But when Roy arrived he was so determined, so obviously eager to get this over with, it was impossible to reason with him. Roy did promise Aaron this would be the last change he'd have while he was at school, but that was all.

Finally, all of Aaron's stuff was packed away in Roy's car.

'Are you sure I can't make you a cup of tea or something?' asked Mum.

'No, no, best be off,' said Roy. 'Traffic's building up.' Roy gave Carrie a hug, shook hands with me and told me 'to look after Mum', after which he gave Mum the tiniest kiss you'd ever seen, looked embarrassed and wandered out to the car. Aaron and I shook hands.

'We wasted so much time,' I said.

'Oh, well, these last two weeks . . . best of my life,' said Aaron. We shook hands again.

'Say goodbye to Laura and Harry for me, won't you?' said Aaron, his voice growing thicker.

'Sure.'

'And Rocky.'

I sprang up. 'I'll get Rocky now,' I said. I brought Rocky downstairs and he immediately jumped on to Aaron's shoulder.

'See you then, Rocky,' croaked Aaron. He had his head lowered, but there was no hiding his tears.

'Aaron's crying,' whispered Carrie.

'Sssh,' muttered Mum.

That night my bedroom seemed very large and very empty. I'd got used to Aaron being there and chatting and having a laugh with him. I remembered what he'd said to me as he left: 'These last two weeks have been the best two weeks of my life.'

They had been the best two weeks of my life too. And now I had to get used to being on my own again. No more Aaron. I buried my face in the pillow and let some tears escape.

That was three weeks ago. Today I got my first letter from Aaron. He told me all about his new school and home. Then, right at the end, he asked about the ghost dog. He'd never seen it since. Had anyone?

Well, Laura and Harry haven't, although I think Laura would half-like to see him.

But I have.

It happened the night Aaron left, actually. I was whistling for him, just as I'd done all those other nights. Then suddenly I cried out, 'Billy, have you really gone? Oh, where are you?'

'I'm right behind you,' said a voice. And there he was. I couldn't believe it.

'But where have you been?'

'I haven't been far away,' said Billy.

'But didn't you hear me calling you all those other nights?'

'I was hiding,' said Billy.

'Hiding!' I exclaimed.

'You humans have a way of creeping into a dog's heart,' said Billy. 'This time I had to be sure.'

'And now?'

Billy didn't reply. He wagged his tail a lot, though, then said, 'Come on, we're wasting time.'

And he led me back to that amazing wood. I fed him there. He was much hungrier this time and his wounds were healing up well. In fact, he said he was feeling so much better he wanted me to throw him some sticks.

So I threw the sticks a little way and Billy proudly brought them back. Then we talked and talked and the sun shone through the trees the whole time. It was just brilliant.

And when I could feel the dream starting to fade I called out, 'Billy, don't hide from me again, will you?'

'Whistle for me and I'll be there,' he called back.

And I know he will. Not as the ghost dog. But as himself, BILLY.

You couldn't dream about a better dog.

THE END

THE CREEPER

Illustrated by David Wyatt

Chapter One

It was horrible.

But I couldn't just walk past it. Somehow, that terrible hand seemed to reach right out of the shop window and pull me closer to it. I stared upwards.

All the skin on the hand had peeled away while its fingertips were cracked and burnt and bent over like a claw.

A truly weird picture.

Below it were two words in shivery, orange writing: *The Creeper*. Then, in much smaller lettering: LISTEN – IF YOU DARE – TO A CLASSIC TALE OF HORROR.

147

I dared. Especially as it was Halloween next Thursday and Amy, my best friend, was sleeping over. My mum had planned a special Halloween meal, but she drew the line at letting us watch horror videos. She and Amy's mum had ganged up together: they went on and on about how most videos just weren't suitable for our age-group. Still, *The Creeper* was a cassette tape so that was all right. I wasn't sure if Mum would agree.

Even so, I decided to buy it quickly while Mum and Dad were across the road looking at some old prints.

Inside the secondhand bookshop a man with a bushy, ginger beard sat at a table, a tray of tea and biscuits beside him. When I asked about *The Creeper* he took a massive gulp of tea, then ambled over to the window.

He picked up the tape, then wiped it on his jacket. I wondered how long it had been in that window. Six months? A year? Ten years? Now I was getting silly. But I liked the idea of *The Creeper* waiting patiently for ages and ages until I came along.

'Sure you want this one?' he asked doubtfully.

I nodded furiously. I just had to have that tape, even if it used up all my spending money. But in the end he only charged me two pounds for it – said it was in the sale.

As I was leaving he called after me, 'Don't listen to that tape on your own, will you?' I think he was trying to be funny.

Outside, to my horror, I bumped straight into Mum. 'Bought something good, Lucy?' She beamed at me.

'I think so.'

Mum undid the paper bag (which the man had carefully sellotaped). 'Oh, Lucy, what's this?'

'It's called a tape, Mum. Haven't

you seen one before? They're quite common now.'

Mum groaned. 'We bring you to London, let you browse around some of the best secondhand bookshops in the country and you buy this trash.'

'You don't know it's trash.' I was indignant.

'Yes I do. Well, you can take it right back.'

'I can't do that,' I said quietly, sulkily. 'I've got to have something spooky for next Thursday. You've banned me from watching videos—'

'I haven't banned you,' interrupted Mum.

'Yes you have. Now you're banning me from listening to tapes. I'm surprised you don't keep me inside all day with a paper bag over my head.'

'Now, that's not fair,' began Mum. Then Dad came over. Mum thrust the tape at him. 'Will you look at what Lucy's just bought?'

He gave a chuckle. 'Well, that hand's well and truly cooked.' Then he read the back and whispered to

Mum, 'I don't think you need worry. Look.'

I couldn't make out what he was pointing at. But it seemed to calm Mum down instantly. A smile slowly formed as she murmured, 'Before even our time,' and handed the tape back to me. 'I suppose it's harmless enough, despite its lurid cover.'

Now I was the one who was worried. It wasn't until I was back at my uncle and aunt's house (where we were staying for the weekend) that I spotted what my dad had seen. It was tucked away right in the corner: FROM THE GOLDEN AGE OF RADIO COLLECTION. FIRST BROADCAST IN 1956.

1956.

I knew the tape would be a few years old but this meant it was medieval, prehistoric. No wonder Mum and Dad weren't bothered. *The Creeper* would probably sound really corny and dated now.

Next day, as soon as we got home, I rushed upstairs to my bedroom and played the start of *The Creeper*.

There was a lot of hissing and crackling at first and my heart began to sink. Then a bell tolled. After which this man started to speak. He sounded ancient.

Greetings and welcome to my horror feast. Tonight I bring another story to chill your spine. But it comes with a special warning: if you are of a nervous disposition or easily scared it is best we say goodbye now.

There was a slight pause while the crackling started up again. Then he returned.

Still here? How brave you must be.
He gave a wheezy laugh. *For this evening I am bringing you face to face with the King of Terror. I dare not say his name aloud. Come a little closer and I shall whisper it to you . . . the Creeper.*

A little chill crept down my spine.

Remember, you can't hide from the Creeper. Wherever you are he will find you. One night, when you are least expecting it, you will hear a tapping noise . . . and it will be the Creeper.

At exactly that moment I heard a tapping sound. I nearly jumped out of my skin. Then my dad put his head round the door. 'Phone call for you, Lucy.' He paused. 'Are you all right, love?'

'Yes, fine,' I said hastily. I didn't want him thinking *The Creeper* was starting to scare me. I switched the tape off and sprinted downstairs.

'It seems ages since I've spoken to you,' said Amy.

'A whole forty-eight hours,' I said.

We speak every night on the phone – even the days we're at school together, to my dad's amazement.

'What have you got left to tell each other?' he exclaimed once. But somehow we never run out of things to say.

'And I suppose,' said Amy, 'you've had a great time in London, while I've been stuck here watching puddles dry.'

'You haven't been out at all then?' I asked. My heart was starting to thump now.

'Well, yesterday the boiler burst, which was sort of exciting. So there's been chaos here ...'

'But you haven't seen ...' I wanted to ask her if she'd seen Natalie, but I changed it to 'anyone'.

'No, because I've had to help my mum ...'

I heaved a sigh of relief. And before I go any further I want to explain something to you. I'm not one of those girls who think their best friend can only have one friend: herself. Truly, I'm not like that. If it was anyone else but Natalie. But I hate Natalie like poison.

She's rich and spoilt, and oh so sly.

She used to have a slave – sorry, friend – named Carla. Natalie would boast away to her for hours and – don't ask me how she did it – but Carla could listen to it all without throwing up once. Then Carla moved away and ever since Natalie has been hunting for a new victim.

Now she's found one: Amy.

Lately she's started showering Amy with stupid little presents. And she makes a big deal of rushing over to Amy first with any news. (Natalie is the biggest gossip in my school.) She's always hanging about with us. But I know I'm surplus to her requirements. And she wants me off the scene so it's just her and Amy.

Yet I can't prove anything without sounding catty and neurotic. Especially as, on the surface, Natalie is nice and friendly to me.

It doesn't help either that I live in this tiny village, miles from anywhere (the average age of its inhabitants is ninety-four), and only see Amy outside school at weekends or on special occasions. While Amy lives quite near the school and so does Natalie. At night I often think about that, wondering if Natalie is round Amy's house now spreading false rumours about me, with a sweet smile on her face as she does so. And sometimes I just can't sleep for worrying. I tell myself I'm being pathetic but I still go on doing it.

Anyway, Amy hadn't seen Natalie that weekend so I heaved a sigh of relief and started telling her about *The Creeper*.

'So what exactly is the Creeper?' asked Amy. 'Is it just a hand?'

'I'm not sure exactly.'

'Maybe that hand scuttles about like a giant spider leaping off curtains at people when they're least expecting it.'

'Can you imagine being attacked by a hand?' I said.

'No, but it sounds excellent just the same,' cried Amy, 'exactly right for Halloween. But you mustn't hear any more of it, otherwise you'll be prepared. I want us to be scared together. Do you promise?'

'Yes, OK,' I replied. 'We'll hear it in my bedroom with just one candle flickering away . . . and I'll decorate my room too.'

'This is going to be so good,' cried Amy.

Later that day I put the tape away in the bottom drawer of my cupboard so I wouldn't be tempted to cheat and play it beforehand.

I was so looking forward to Halloween night.

But in the end nothing turned out as I'd expected.

Chapter Two

The next few days at school were
ghastly – thanks to Natalie. Whenever I turned round there she was,
pulling Amy away to whisper some
rubbish in her ear.

Once I said to Amy, 'It'll be nice to
have a conversation one day without
Natalie butting in,' but she just
smiled and said, 'Oh, Natalie's all
right.' Amy seemed so different these
days. She was changing into another
person; someone who was more
Natalie's friend than mine.

And I didn't know what to do about
it. Then, on Thursday afternoon,
something really bad happened.

Amy and I were walking out of school, when surprise, surprise, Natalie turned up and hissed, 'Oh, Amy, can you come into town with me tomorrow after school? You've got to say yes, as I need your help. You see, I've got to buy . . .'

I couldn't bear to listen to another word and slunk away. But I decided that when Amy came round to hear *The Creeper* tonight, I'd tell her how I was sick of Natalie trying to push me out all the time. Amy was just going to have to choose between Natalie and me.

Amy called out my name. But I didn't turn round. There was no way I could say a word to her with Natalie's big ears flapping.

Right now I just wanted to go home.

Usually my mum picked me up from school (there's only about one bus a year to my village and that's always late) but occasionally, if my dad finished work early, he'd turn up instead. Today was one of those days. He obviously didn't think I'd seen him because he was parked quite a way down the road from the school. So he got out of the car and yelled my name as if I were lost at sea or something.

That was embarrassing enough, but worse, much worse, was to follow. You won't believe what he was wearing.

He still had on the suit jacket he wore to work but underneath it – amazingly, bafflingly – were his red tracksuit bottoms. Now my dad's tracksuit is an eyesore at the best of times, but worn with his suit jacket it plunged new depths of awfulness.

I called out to him, hoping he'd quickly get back in the car again and hide himself away. But no, he carried on leaning against the car, revealing to everyone his appalling taste in clothes.

Of course Natalie had to say, 'What is your dad wearing, Lucy?'

I didn't answer. But I knew I was turning bright red. I could hear Natalie and Amy whispering about my dad. Then Amy said, 'He dresses like a prat.' And they were both killing themselves laughing.

How dare Amy be so disloyal. And how dare she sneer at my dad just to keep in with Natalie. My dad's always been really nice to her and given her masses of lifts. A terrible fury burned inside me.

Then, before I knew what was happening, this bitter, sarcastic voice I hardly recognized as my own said something to Amy which was unforgivably nasty. Immediately I regretted what I'd said. I wanted to pull back the words. But I couldn't. All I could do was stand there staring at Amy.

And she didn't seem angry, not at first. There was just this look of total amazement on her face as if she couldn't quite believe what I'd done. But I could feel the shock and horror running through her. Then her face seemed to crumple and she turned away from me.

Natalie, who'd been watching all this open-mouthed, suddenly put an arm around Amy and led her away. But not before she'd flashed me a little smile of triumph. My outburst had played right into her hands.

I ran across the road to my dad, who was wiping the windscreen with a cloth. He hadn't heard what had just happened and smiled cheerfully at me. 'I didn't even have time to change properly before your mum was pushing me out of the door. She said you worry if we're late.'

And it was true – the few times my mum had been late I did worry, imagining all sorts of dire fates for her.

'Well, I left your mum getting ready for your Halloween night. I expect you're looking forward to that.'

'Oh yes,' I said, still in a daze. I practically fell into Dad's car. He chatted the whole way back. I replied without really listening to anything he said.

I can't tell you how much I regretted what I'd just said to Amy. It was something which I knew she'd find very hurtful. But for a moment there I totally lost it. It was as if all the anger which had been bubbling up inside me for days suddenly boiled over.

It was just lucky no-one else had heard me – except Natalie. Still, Natalie knowing was like putting it on the news.

What a complete mess.

But then I told myself it wasn't all my fault. Amy shouldn't have called my dad a prat. Only I can call him that. I had the right to defend my dad – and retaliate. I kept repeating this to myself without ever quite believing it.

In the end I didn't know what to think. I felt all knotted up inside.

Back home my mum brought this hollowed-out pumpkin up to my room, then fixed a candle in the middle of it. 'That should help create the atmosphere you want tonight,' she said.

'Great. Thanks, Mum.'

'When will Amy be coming round?'

'About half-six.' That was the time we'd decided earlier in the day. But would Amy be coming at all now? I knew she was very keen to hear *The Creeper*. But after what I'd just said to her surely she wouldn't show up. Or maybe she'd realize I'd been goaded into saying that, and she'd call round to clear the air between us.

In a kind of trance I started getting my room ready. I smeared fake blood all down my mirror and sprayed cobwebby stuff over my wardrobe. Dad had bought these bats – all ten of them.

'Just put three or four up on the ceiling,' said Mum.

But in the end Dad and I pinned them all up, so they were like a small army above my head.

'Doesn't this room look gruesome?' Dad grinned conspiratorially at me.

Then Mum brought up a tray of sandwiches. She had stuck plastic spiders all over them. 'I'm sure you and Amy will have much more fun tonight than you would watching those awful videos. If you get through all those sandwiches, just shout . . . Now, I suppose I'd better get ready for our friends.'

Two couples were joining Mum and Dad for a meal tonight. They took it in turns to go round to each other's houses. Sometimes I wondered if that would be Amy and me in twenty years' time: still seeing each other on Friday nights but with our husbands too. We'd even laughed together about that.

'I expect Amy will be here any minute,' said Mum. 'Don't eat all the sandwiches before she comes, will you?'

But I knew I wouldn't be able to manage even one of them. I felt sick with anxiety. I really hoped Amy would come round tonight so we could sort this out.

We were best friends, after all. Hadn't she given me a chain with half a heart and BEST written on it. She had the other half of the heart with FRIEND on it. The two halves fitted together perfectly.

I was dead excited when she gave me that chain. You see, before Amy started at our school I'd never had a best friend.

I had friends, of course, but no-one special, no-one I confided in. Mum said it must be difficult for me living so far away from the school. That was true. But it was also an excuse. I was very shy (still am, really). And in a way I quite liked being by myself. Dad said once that I lived in a world of my own. Occasionally that world got a bit lonely but I also felt happy and safe there.

At school I'd make up things I'd done at the weekend. I'd invent friends I'd seen, too. Only it didn't feel as if I were lying, because I could see it all so clearly in my head. I was just telling stories, really.

One time I told my class I'd been to a film première. That wasn't a complete lie. You see, my mum writes reviews for the local paper and once she got tickets for an advance preview of a film. I was dead excited, I really thought I was going to the première, but instead we were escorted into this tiny room where we watched the film with a few other people from the local press, and had a few stale sandwiches afterwards.

It was so disappointing. But at school on Monday I described the première in such detail – as well as all the stars who were there – that everyone believed me, except Natalie: she said they didn't have premières at the weekend.

Natalie was nasty even then. And she was incredibly spiteful to Amy when she first started at our school. You see, Amy was very shy and quiet and always looked as if she were about to burst into tears, so everyone wrote her off as a boring swot, except me. I knew there was much more to her than that.

We started going round together. Soon I was discovering how funny Amy could be – she did wicked impressions – and we had so much in common too.

First it was obvious things, like neither of us having any brothers or sisters. But then there were eerie coincidences: for instance, in

February, before she joined our school, Amy's cat, which she loved, was run over. Well, amazingly, on almost the same day, my brilliant dog Benji also died, though in his case of old age.

We weren't just friends, we were more like long-lost twins. Even though we don't look much alike: I'm quite tall and dark-haired while Amy is very small and blonde. But when I had my hair cut short, so did Amy just a few days later, which I thought was a real compliment. It was all going so well until Natalie . . .

'It's gone seven o'clock.' My mum stood in the doorway. 'Do you want to give Amy a call?'

No I didn't, because I had a horrible feeling she would slam the phone down on me. She wasn't coming, was she?

'No, I won't, Mum.' I ached to tell Mum the truth. But I couldn't. It was too shaming. 'Actually, Amy's not sure her mum will allow her out tonight.'

'Oh, no.' Mum sounded really upset. 'How about if I give her mum a call?' Our mums got on well so it seemed a good suggestion, but not tonight.

'No,' I said quickly. 'You see, Amy and her mum have had an argument. Quite a bad one, actually.'

'Do you know what it was about?'

'Not really. Amy didn't go into the details. She was hoping her mum might let her out tonight but . . .' I shrugged my shoulders and sighed.

'Well why not come downstairs?

It's just boring old grown-ups, I'm afraid, but we'll try and entertain you for a bit. Might even tell a few ghost stories.'

'It's all right, Mum. I think I'll still play my tape.'

'You can tell Amy what she missed on Monday.'

'That's right.'

Mum squeezed my hand. 'But what a pity when you've gone to all this trouble too.'

I turned my head away. 'Ah well, more sandwiches for me, I suppose.'

But Mum wasn't fooled. She stayed chatting for a few more minutes. Then Dad came in. They only left when the doorbell went and the first of their guests arrived.

Outside the wind cried and screamed. Even the weather seemed to be angry tonight. I drew the curtains and switched the light off. There was just one candle lighting up the room. I placed *The Creeper* beside it. That hand looked even more menacing now.

I'd waited all week to hear this

story. I wasn't going to wait any longer. And I wasn't going to let Amy spoil any more of tonight, either. If she'd come round I'm sure we could have sorted everything out. A real friend would have done that. She was obviously sulking: well, let her. I didn't care.

But just then the doorbell rang again and I knew it couldn't be Amy – not now – but I wished with all my heart it was.

I sat down on my swing chair and listened. It was hard to make out anything. But I couldn't hear Amy's voice.

I closed my eyes and swung round and round. I whirled so fast I started to feel sick. All at once I could hear footsteps coming up the stairs. My bedroom door opened.

A boy in a Dracula cape stood in the doorway.

'Trick or treat,' he said.

Chapter Three

I blinked at him in astonishment.

For a moment I didn't recognize Jack.

But then he had painted his face white, and gelled his hair back. And he was wearing a white shirt, black bow-tie and black trousers.

He waved his fangs at me. 'They kept falling out so I thought it'd be easier to carry them.' He looked at me. 'It was all right to just come up . . . ?'

'Yeah, sure, of course. It's good to see you.'

Jack is the only person roughly my age (he's a year and a bit older than me) who lives nearby. A while back he was often round my house. But since I'd become friendly with Amy we'd drifted apart a bit.

'Have you been round the village dressed like that?' I asked.

'I have.'

'How much money did you make then?'

Jack dug into his pocket. 'Twenty-five pence and three Quality Street.'

He looked so indignant I burst out laughing.

He went on, 'The women are OK, you can have a joke with them. It's the men who always slam the door really hard. One threatened me with a bucket of water. Can you believe that?'

'Well I think you look great,' I said.

'So do I.'

I suddenly remembered when I'd last seen Jack. It was just after Benji, my dog, had died. He came round several times. He'd been a real friend then.

Jack started prowling around. He tapped my mirror with the fake blood on it. 'That's wicked . . . your bedroom's really improved. You should always keep it like this. So are you expecting anyone else?'

'Amy,' I said quickly. Jack didn't go to my school and had never met Amy. Suddenly I was glad about that. 'But I don't think she can make it now.'

'That's a shame.' But he didn't sound very sad.

'We were going to play a tape.' I picked up *The Creeper*.

He squinted at the cover. 'That looks really gross – slap it on.' He settled himself down in the swing chair, depositing his fangs on one of the arms. I sat on my bed. He grinned at me.

Jack has the look of a naughty boy, the one who's always kept behind in detention. He's usually scruffy, has a blob nose, large green eyes and a big infectious laugh. He couldn't have picked a better time to call round.

The tape crackled and started. 'I've been waiting so long to play this,' I said. 'Amy wanted to hear it with me.'

I suddenly wondered what she was doing now. Was she thinking about our falling-out? Or was she chatting on the phone to Natalie?

'Which century is this tape from?' called out Jack.

I smiled. 'It's a classic.'

'Says who?'

I heard again that elderly voice say:

I am bringing you face to face with the King of Terror. I dare not say his name aloud. Come a little closer and I shall whisper it to you . . . the Creeper.

The Creeper wasn't always a monster. Once he was an ordinary, kind human being called Martin Sloane, who lived in a small cottage on a farm with just Rusty, a spaniel, for company. He often helped the elderly farmer and when the old man died he left a third of the farm to him. His two sons, Jeremiah and Jethro, were furious.

'Jeremiah and Jethro. Those names are too stupid to mention,' cried Jack.

'They were probably really cool names in their day,' I replied.

'No way.'

'Sssh.'

Together the brothers plotted something evil. A few nights later Rusty disappeared. Martin thought Rusty might be in the barn searching for mice. He rushed inside. The next thing he knew the barn door had slammed shut behind him – and the hay was alight with fire.

'He's going to be toasted alive,' cried Jack gleefully. 'Excellent.'

Martin pounded on the door, his cries growing more and more desperate. But Rusty heard her master. She broke free from the brothers who'd captured her, and tore outside to the barn. She scratched frantically at the door. But her master's cries grew fainter and fainter, until finally she couldn't hear him at all.

The brothers raised the alarm. But by now Martin had crumbled away. All that was left of him were his ashes, and one red and blistered hand. It was the end of Martin (the story-teller's voice dropped) *but just the beginning of the Creeper. For something moved in the smoke and darkness: something which could not be destroyed.*

A tiny glimmer of fire glowed with a strange, unearthly brilliance. The air suddenly seemed to grow thicker. Martin's ashes rustled and stirred.

Suddenly, that piece of fire shot into the air shining fiercely. It acted as a magnet for all those pieces of dust, which rose up around it and then assembled themselves into the shape of a human.

Finally, that claw-like hand joined this man made of ashes and fire.

He was called 'The Creeper'.

His first steps out of the fire were slow and unsteady as he struggled to get used to his new legs. But as he made his way through the night he made an incredible discovery: he didn't have to walk at all; now he could float through the air like smoke. The dark night acted as camouflage so no-one saw the Creeper brush past them, though some people wondered how they could suddenly smell burning, and at the rush of heat they felt.

But wherever the Creeper went he left a small trail of dust behind him.

'Well, the Creeper wouldn't have lasted a minute in my house,' burst out Jack. 'My mum would have hoovered him up. No problem.'

I gave another small laugh in reply. While the story wasn't scaring me, exactly, it was making me feel a bit uneasy. Especially that bit about the dust all rising up. I hadn't liked that. I hoped I wouldn't dream about it tonight.

The story went on:

The Creeper began to plot his revenge against the brothers. That night he could do nothing because of his one enemy: the rain. He took shelter against its hateful powers.

'Shouldn't think he has many baths then,' quipped Jack.

But the following night was clear and cool. Jeremiah slept in his room, dreaming of all the money he was going to inherit. Then he stirred

uneasily. He could hear something. A faint tapping on his window. Tap, tap, tap.

Jeremiah decided it was just the wind. But he slept badly. The following night he was again disturbed. He thought he heard someone whispering his name. 'The Creeper knows,' said a voice. Jeremiah sat straight up. Then he uttered a scream of terror at the figure standing at the foot of his bed. He rubbed his eyes, certain that this must be a nightmare. And the figure seemed to vanish instantly.

But next day all Jeremiah could think about was his nightmare. By nightfall he had become agitated and upset. He dreaded having that dream again. And sure enough, in the middle of the night, he saw someone standing there in his bedroom once more.

He rubbed his eyes but this time he couldn't make the stranger disappear. Instead he went on standing there, his dark, orange eyes filled with steely menace. Jeremiah's skin began to creep.

He wasn't the only one. There was something disturbing about this tale. I was sure Amy would have found it scary. She'd have sat with her arm around me whispering and giggling softly. At least Jack was here. I looked across at him. He immediately pretended to be biting his nails with fear.

The music grew louder and so did the story-teller's voice.

'Don't you recognize me, Jeremiah?' asked the Creeper. Tiny particles of dust shot out of his mouth every time he spoke.

Jeremiah began to splutter, 'It was an accident.'

The Creeper shook his head angrily. 'Do not try my patience. I know your guilty secret. But remember, there's no hiding place from the Creeper.'

Jeremiah was trembling all over now. 'Look, I'll give you anything, all you want.'

'What good is money to me now?' He gave a strange kind of wheezy laugh, then raised his hand as if to ward off a terrible blow.

At the sight of the Creeper's hand Jeremiah let out a gasp, and the only words he could utter were: 'Mercy, mercy.'

'Mercy,' echoed the Creeper contemptuously. 'Don't you know you have turned my heart to dust too?' Then he slipped away, leaving Jeremiah so terror-stricken he could not even speak for several weeks.

Next it was time for the Creeper to pay his first visit to Jethro. He was still awake, going through the account books in his study. He whistled tunelessly to himself, not hearing at first the tapping noise on his window. Tap, tap, tap.

Almost immediately came a faint tapping noise from my window too, like a weird kind of echo. I looked across at Jack.

And then the candle went out.

Chapter Four

My room was in darkness. I gave a little gasp which I quickly turned into a laugh. 'So who blew the candle out?'

'The Creeper,' said Jack. 'It must be his birthday.'

We both laughed a little too loudly.

On the tape the Creeper was paying Jethro a second visit and declaring, *'There is no escape from the Creeper.'*

Strange how much louder those words sounded in the dark. Then came that tapping noise against my window again.

That sounded louder too.

'Tell Mr Creeper to come in and make himself at home,' said Jack.

Now my curtains were moving, just as if they were letting someone in.

'I'm going to put the light on,' I announced.

Jack didn't argue.

The switch was right in the corner of my room by the door. I groped my way along the wall. My hand went out, then I snapped it back as if someone had just bitten it.

For something was now on my hand.

'Jack,' I gasped. 'Something's landed on me. I can feel it moving.'

He was beside me in an instant, squinting into the darkness. 'Where is it?'

'On my hand,' I cried. 'I told you that.'

'All right, take it easy. Did you find the light switch?'

Trembling now, my hand reached out again. A moment later my bedroom was full of pale, yellow light.

I looked down. One of the bats

which Dad and I had carefully stuck up on the ceiling now lay on my hand.

'All right,' I said to Jack, who was killing himself laughing. 'It was just the way it suddenly plonked down on to me.'

'*I can feel it moving*,' mimicked Jack.

I threw the bat at him. And he immediately pretended to stamp on it. From the tape came a horrible kind of gurgle from Jethro, followed by a strange whooshing noise as the Creeper flew out of Jethro's window.

'What a stupid sound-effect,' began Jack. Then he stopped as we heard another sound-effect. Once more something was tapping or scratching against the window.

We dashed across my room. I pulled back the curtains and stared out at a dark blue sky. The wind raged on, making the branches of the cherry tree by the window swing about wildly.

Jack pointed at the tree. 'There's your mysterious caller . . . it was just the wind.'

'That's what Jeremiah thought,' I blurted out. Immediately I felt ashamed for saying something so daft and smiled as if I'd made a joke.

Then Mum called, 'Everything all right up there?'

'Yes, fine thanks,' I called back.

'You didn't tell her the Creeper came knocking,' teased Jack.

'You're so funny.' The tape clicked off. 'Do you want to hear the other side?'

'No, that old prune's voice is getting on my nerves.'

I fumbled about for the off-switch; my hand was still shaking.

'You'd better sit down before you fall down,' said Jack, not unkindly.

We both sat on the side of my bed. Jack began to laugh again. 'Are you laughing at me?' I asked.

'I can't help it.'

'I wasn't really scared, you know.'

Jack's eyebrows shot up about two feet.

'It was just the weird coincidence of my tree tapping against the window at exactly the same time as . . .'

'I believe you,' said Jack mockingly.

'You can be so annoying sometimes.'

'Only sometimes? I'm slipping.'

'Anyway, I noticed you were sitting pretty still during some parts of that story.'

Jack spluttered with indignation. 'What! Now listen, if I was sitting still it was because I was gobsmacked by how far-fetched the whole thing was. I mean, what's the plot? This guy's ashes get up and turn into a bloke who can fly. Then he zaps off and terrorizes people with his magic hand, which you just have to look at and *wham*, you're speechless.' He shook his head. 'That is a pathetic story, totally pathetic. And as for those five-penny special effects: like that whooshing noise the Creeper makes. You know how they do that, don't you? It's just someone blowing into a milk bottle.'

I smiled. 'Really.'

'Oh yeah, it's dead primitive. And those sounds of fire: they were so obviously jammed in from somewhere else.' He stretched. 'Still, I wouldn't mind if the Creeper came to call on me.' He gave a sly grin. 'Actually, it'd be really useful because my bedroom's freezing at night . . . and he'd soon warm it up, wouldn't he?'

I was laughing now. Then we both started making up silly jokes about the Creeper or 'Dust-breath', as Jack called him.

And yet, I still had this nagging worry about the tapping noise we'd heard.

Of course, it probably *had* been caused by the wind. But I couldn't remember it ever happening before.

Still, the wind was particularly wild tonight – and anyway, what else could it be?

Jack got up. 'I suppose I'd better go or my mum will be sending out a search party. Shame it's school tomorrow.'

'I know. Well, thanks for coming round. Come back any time,' I added.

'I might just do that.' Jack stopped and turned round. 'Mustn't forget my fangs.' He picked them up from the arm of the chair, put them in and grinned at me. 'I'd better run home now before the Creeper gets me.'

Chapter Five

That night I dreamt about the Creeper – and Jack. I saw Jack running out of this wood. He yelled to me, 'Don't go down there, the Creeper's waiting for his next victim.' At that moment I saw Amy strolling into the wood. I called out. She turned round and I shouted a warning.

She just looked straight through me and then carried on.

I was still screaming at her to stop when I woke up. I couldn't get off to sleep again. But it wasn't the Creeper who was keeping me awake. It was Amy.

I lay there in the dark wishing I hadn't said such cruel things to her, and in front of Natalie, too. If only I'd kept my anger under control. If only . . . I felt awful.

My guilt was like a great heavy weight right on the top of my stomach. There was only one way I could make it go away.

I started to plan out my apology: Amy usually got to school early. We'd often meet up by the coat pegs outside our classroom. So first thing tomorrow I'd be there with *The Creeper* under my arm. I'd go up to Amy and say, as she missed hearing the story last night, would she like to borrow it now? Then, having broken the ice I'd dive into a full apology. I practised that over and over. I was still begging her forgiveness when I fell asleep.

Then, what seemed like only two minutes later Mum was shaking me awake. My whole body ached with tiredness and my throat felt sore. I wondered if I was going to be ill. Well, not yet. I had to see Amy first.

Downstairs I had no appetite. But Mum said she couldn't let me go to school with nothing inside me. I forced down a piece of toast. Mum asked me if I was feeling all right.

'Just great,' I replied.

I got Mum to drop me off at school early. I made straight for the coat pegs outside my classroom. It was deserted. I stood waiting. I felt like an actress waiting for a play to start.

Heidi, a girl in my form, appeared with her mum. 'I've lost my new pen,' she muttered. They searched around. I helped them. None of us could find it. Then Heidi and her grim-faced mum went off to our classroom. I heard Heidi's mum say, 'Well, I'm not buying you another one.'

Then I spotted Amy. I walked towards her, but my heart sank. She was not alone. Natalie was with her.

Usually Natalie was late for school, but not today. I wondered if she'd guessed I'd try and see Amy now and that was why she was here.

We drew nearer. Then Natalie called out, 'Amy trusted you. I can't believe what you said to her yesterday. It was so cruel.'

'Just get lost, will you?' I began. But then I added, 'You didn't believe what I said about Amy yesterday, did you? You knew it was all made up.'

'Oh, I know you're a complete liar,' said Natalie. 'I haven't forgotten when you tried to pretend you went to that film première.'

I shot Amy a look as if to say, well at least Natalie didn't believe what I said yesterday, but Amy didn't react at all. She just stood there looking thin and sad.

'This is between Amy and me,' I said, glaring at Natalie.

'Amy wants me to stay,' said Natalie. 'And so I will.'

I took a deep breath, then dug into my bag. I held up *The Creeper*.

'What is that?' exclaimed Natalie.

'It looks disgusting.'

I ignored her. 'Amy, I'm really sorry you missed *The Creeper* last night. I know you wanted to hear it, so please borrow it, and keep it as long as you like.' I had that part off by heart. I looked at Amy expectantly.

But she didn't do anything except give me this horrible dead stare, eerily similar to the one in my dream last night. My voice rose a couple of notches. 'Amy, I just wanted to say . . .'

All at once Amy turned on me. 'I don't know why you're talking to me. If I were you I'd go off and find a new best friend because I just don't want to know you any more.'

I gave a gasp as if I'd just swallowed a piece of ice. I felt scared and lost.

'And Amy wants her chain back,' cut in Natalie.

That gave me a stab of pain all right. 'You didn't say that, did you?' I was pleading with Amy now. She didn't answer. But her pale blue eyes had narrowed to tiny pinpricks.

Blinking away tears I flung the chain down in front of Amy and Natalie. 'Have your precious chain. I never want to speak to you again.'

I tore off, nearly colliding with Heidi and her mum. Heidi beamed at me. 'We found my pen. It was—'

'That's great,' I interrupted and fled towards the playground. All around me people were arriving. Some of them watched in surprise as I rushed out of school.

'I wonder what she's forgotten,'

asked one woman, then laughed, as if she'd made a joke.

I ran right up the road from my school, then stopped and sat down on a wall outside someone's house.

Amy never even gave me a chance to explain. At least she owed me that. But Natalie's obviously taken her over completely now. And when I go into the classroom I know Amy will have moved and she'll be sitting next to Natalie, just as Natalie had planned all along.

I could just go away and hide somewhere. But I'd only get into more trouble, and wouldn't Natalie love that. Besides, my head was hot and throbbing.

I got up and slowly walked back to school. I looked at my watch. Nine o'clock. Mrs Cole would be taking the register now. I was officially late.

Suddenly I heard someone calling my name: 'Lucy Chandler.' Mrs Walker, the school secretary, was advancing towards me. Everyone made fun of her awful lace-up shoes and thick stockings but everyone was scared of her too, even the teachers.

'You should be in Mrs Cole's class now, not strolling into school.' She studied me; her tone softened. 'Are you all right, Lucy?'

'No, Mrs Walker, I'm not.' That wasn't a lie. I did feel groggy.

'Were you feeling well before you left home this morning?'

She started firing questions at me. Did I feel tired, shivery? Then she asked, 'And does your throat feel as if you've swallowed a lot of dust?'

For a moment that made me think of the Creeper. A shiver ran through me. 'Yes, my throat feels exactly like that.' And it did.

'Well, you'll have to go home for observation. Come with me.' She marched off to her office. I had to half-run to keep up with her.

She rang up my mum but there was no answer. 'I think she might be out doing an interview,' I said. 'She'll be back soon, though.'

Mrs Walker nodded. 'You'd better lie down there.' She pointed at a black, iron bed in the corner of her room. It looked just like a prison bed. I went to scramble on to it.

'Take your shoes off first,' commanded Mrs Walker in shocked tones.

'Oh yes, sorry.'

'Would you like a glass of water?' she asked.

I shook my head.

'Well, I'd better let Mrs Cole know where you are.'

I closed my eyes. To my surprise I slept for a while. When I woke up I heard Mrs Walker talking on the phone. I sat up, not knowing where I was at first.

'Ah, just been talking about you,' she said. 'Your mother's on her way over.'

Mum fussed over me in the car, even putting a rug around me. As soon as we got home she took my temperature.

'What is it?' I asked.

Mum patted my arm. 'It's a little bit higher than usual. I'm afraid you've caught this bug that's going around.'

At first it was a relief to climb into bed and know I had a proper reason to escape seeing Natalie and Amy together. I wondered what Amy would say when she found out I'd gone home, ill. Would she wish she'd been a bit nicer to me, and feel guilty? Maybe she'd even ring me tonight to see how I was. But then I could hear Natalie saying, 'Lucy's not really ill. She's pretending as usual.'

And Amy never rang.

Then I decided if Amy didn't want to be friends with me any more that was fine. From now on she wasn't part of my life either. And I wouldn't waste another second thinking about her.

Over the weekend my headache got worse. I was hot and sweaty all the time and could hardly even walk to the loo. And I kept sleeping in little bursts, the way very old people do.

By Monday I was getting restless. The headache had gone off but I still felt very weak. Dad played cards with me. And Mum bought me all these comics and magazines I don't normally get. She also let me borrow her portable television. But after a while even the good programmes seemed like rubbish.

My eyes hurt too much to read for very long. So I was feeling decidedly bored one afternoon when my gaze alighted on *The Creeper*. I was curious to hear how it ended.

Then I dared myself to play it.

Thin November sunshine was trickling through my window. There were no candles to blow out, all my Halloween decorations were down. *The Creeper* couldn't possibly scare me now.

That was what I thought.

Chapter Six

The beginning of the next Creeper story was about his dog, Rusty. I'd wondered what had happened to her. Well, it turned out the villagers had gathered up some of what they thought were Martin's ashes and made a little grave for him. Some kind people had taken Rusty in. But every night she scraped at the door until they let her go and sit by her master's grave. She would stay there all night, howling. 'That dog is breaking her heart,' the people said.

The story continued:

One cold winter's night the dog looked up to see something moving in the darkness. She gave a low, warning growl. The figure stirred. Then Rusty gave a yelp of joy, dancing all around the figure.

'You still know me, don't you, girl,' said the Creeper. 'But come, follow me.'

She had not eaten well since her master had died, and she moved somewhat unsteadily.

The Creeper stopped at the house where Rusty now lived. 'It's too cold for you to be out at night. Don't do it again.'

Rusty saw her master move away. She started to follow him. 'No,' said the Creeper. 'This is your home now. I've been watching them for a while. I know they will look after you well here.'

Still Rusty wouldn't leave the Creeper's side.

'Go away,' hissed the Creeper. 'I don't want you any more. Do you understand? Now, clear off. Forget me.' His voice broke with emotion. 'I don't want you.'

I felt really sorry for the Creeper

having to give up his dog. But soon he was back on the revenge trail again.

No-one saw the Creeper gliding through the night or staring through their windows. Once he saw a sight which enraged him: a man hitting his little puppy.

The Creeper began visiting the man: first by tapping on his window, then appearing briefly, and finally declaring: 'I know what wrong you have done.' The man's eyes shot open, then he reached out for his gun. He'd kept it beside his bed ever since these strange occurrences had started.

'No gun can kill me.' The Creeper gave a strange, creaky laugh. 'Nothing can stop me.' From out of the darkness a figure moved towards the man. It was the eyes he saw first: orange and staring.

Then the Creeper raised his terrible hand. The man found his body suddenly weak. 'Mercy,' he squeaked. 'Mercy.'

'What mercy did you show your poor puppy?' whispered the Creeper. The man no longer had enough breath even to splutter. And then he lay completely still, his eyes bulging with horror. The Creeper moved with the swiftness of lightning. As always, the only clue he left behind were tiny pieces of dust on the window sill.

The Creeper had been haunting someone else: a young man who had stolen money from his two brothers and business partners. When the Creeper confronted him he cried out in amazement, 'But how do you know all this?'

'Even when you think you are alone, the Creeper sees.'

The man begged for another chance. This time the Creeper relented. 'Remember, you may not see me but I shall be there . . . watching you. You cannot hide from the Creeper. Now go and return the money you have stolen.'

Then the young man, still wiping the sweat from his forehead, rushed out and did just that, stuffing envelopes full of money through his brothers' doors at two o'clock in the morning.

The tape ended abruptly with the words, *So remember, even when you are alone, the Creeper sees.*

Outside the sun had gone and the darkness seemed to be rushing at my window. I nestled down in bed imagining the Creeper skulking unseen, like a ghost by day and then at night leaping out on the wrong-doers. What a shock it must have been for people to wake up and spot the Creeper there.

Still, it was only a story and a very old one too. I wished, though, I hadn't heard it on my own. If only Amy had been here too. In the past we'd had the odd argument. But then we'd just look at each other and laugh. Our friendship was stronger than any stupid row. But this time it was different. I'd really hurt her. I'd . . .

But I couldn't bear to think about what I'd done to my best friend. I closed my eyes tightly. Then my mum came in with some hot soup. I felt each mouthful go all the way down. It was as if my throat was on fire.

Later I drifted off to sleep. It was the middle of the night when I woke again. I thought I'd heard a tapping noise. I must have been dreaming. I turned over on my side. My head felt all hot and clammy.

Then I received the biggest shock of my life.

. A voice, so close he could have been standing beside me, whispered, 'You cannot hide from the Creeper.'

Chapter Seven

I shot up in bed. My room was wrapped in darkness. It was like a great thick wall, which at first I couldn't see over. A glimmer of light slid through my curtains from the street lights outside. I peered around me.

Every muscle in my body had tensed up. I sensed danger. And then I saw a shape over by the wardrobe.

Someone was standing there.

The Creeper.

I couldn't move, I couldn't even breathe. A scream was forming in my mouth. Then I fell back on my pillows, weak with relief.

I knew who that figure was.

My wardrobe door has never closed properly. Sometimes it will stay shut for hours, then jump open when you're least expecting it – usually at night, too. That's why I leave it slightly ajar all the time now. And my winter coat was hanging over the side of the door. I gave a half-laugh. How silly I'd been. But in the dark my coat looked just like a small, watchful person.

Yet there was still the voice I'd heard. The Creeper's voice. Was he hiding somewhere in the shadows? I searched with my eyes.

My bedroom changed at night: everything became hostile, alien. Those toys peering over the top of my cupboard certainly weren't on my side now. They stared at me suspiciously. And the people on my posters who grinned at me throughout the day had all lost their smiles, and most of their faces too. Everything had become shadowy and sinister.

But I was all alone, wasn't I? Nothing stirred in here except my curtains. They swayed in and out because I'd left the window slightly open. I like some fresh air at night.

So fresh air was the only thing creeping into my room. Yet I couldn't make myself believe that. I kept scanning my room while the words I'd heard were still echoing around my head. Something had spoken, so something must be in here unless . . . unless the tape switched on by itself. No, that was impossible. But how else could I explain it?

I closed my eyes for a moment. And then I heard it again, its words cutting through the darkness: 'The Creeper knows your guilty secret.'

Terror put wings on my feet. I just flew out of my bedroom. Then I stood tottering on the landing, breathing in gulps. I saw someone coming towards me.

My dad was approaching me the way you might a wild animal. 'Hello, Lucy, it's your dad.' His voice was low and reassuring. He obviously thought I was sleep-walking and didn't want to alarm me.

'I'm awake, Dad, and there's something in my room. I heard it speaking.'

'Well, let's go and see, shall we?'

I shrank back.

'Come on, we'll check your room together.' He stretched out his hand to me. I grabbed hold of it and we walked slowly back into my bedroom. Dad put the light on and said, 'Now, you get into bed while I check it out.'

I sat up in bed while Dad prowled slowly around my room. I knew he was just humouring me, but I still watched him intently. He tried to close my wardrobe door.

'Don't close it, Dad, it will only come open again.'

'All right, although I would think that coat hanging there would be enough to scare anyone.'

'Will you unplug the tape recorder for me?'

'Certainly.' Dad bounded over and removed the plug. 'Now, anything else you'd like me to do?'

'I'm not wasting your time. I did hear something, you know.'

'Of course you did.' He sat down on the edge of the bed. 'Dreams can seem very real. Remember when you kept running downstairs convinced there was a dinosaur hiding in the kitchen cupboard?'

We chatted and I laughed about that for a while. Then he said, 'I expect you're feeling sleepy now, aren't you?'

'Sort of.'

'Shall I leave the light on?'

I shook my head. I can't sleep if the light's on.

'Now, if you hear anything else just

shout and I'll be in right away. OK?'

I snuggled down in bed. While he was here Dad almost convinced me it had been a dream. But as soon as he'd gone my doubts came crashing back.

I was certainly awake when I heard the Creeper's voice the second time. And you can't dream when you're awake, can you?

So what had caused it?

I looked down at my tape recorder. Somehow it had managed to switch itself on. That must be the explanation. Still, it was unplugged now so nothing else weird could happen, except . . . with a stab of horror, I realized the Creeper tape was still lurking inside there.

All at once I got up, yanked *The Creeper* out of the tape recorder and flung it in the bottom drawer of my dressing table. I shoved it right at the back, too. Then I whispered, 'Try switching yourself on from there, Dust-breath.'

Chapter Eight

'My TV went mad once,' said Jack.

'What happened?' I asked, leaning forward.

'Well, late one night I was lying in bed watching telly when it suddenly started changing channels all by itself.' He paused dramatically. 'That telly only worked by remote control, which was right beside me and I hadn't touched it. But the TV kept on jumping from channel to channel just as if some invisible force were operating it.' He stopped pacing around my room and half-whispered, 'Then the lights started to dim.'

'What did you do?'

'Ran like mad downstairs . . . But that was ages ago now,' he added hastily. 'I was only about five at the time.'

'And what had caused it?'

'Something to do with a power surge. I don't remember exactly. But that could be what made your tape switch itself on last night.' He bent down and peered at me. 'You look dead pale, by the way. Do you feel dead pale?'

I nodded. This morning my temperature had shot up. Mum didn't tell me that. But I heard her and Dad whispering about it outside. Then the doctor turned up. He stuck a cold and clammy hand on my forehead and said, 'Well, you've got yourself a few more days off school, young lady.' Then he told me off for not drinking enough fluids.

Still, I was too busy being groggy to think much about the Creeper during the day. It was only as it grew darker outside that he popped back in my head. That's why I was so glad when Jack appeared. Even though I knew my hair had gone all manky, and I looked sweaty and horrible.

He stretched out on my swing chair and said, 'The other rational explanation is that you dreamt the whole thing.'

'That's what my dad reckons.'

'Well, you were listening to Dustbreath just before you went to sleep, weren't you?'

I nodded. 'You can borrow the tape and hear the rest of it if you like.'

'I'd sooner staple my nostrils together. Just tell me the highlights – if there were any.'

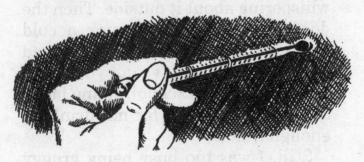

I began to recount what happened on side two. Jack was soon exclaiming, 'Really, the Creeper's nothing more than a peeping tom looking through people's windows all the time. Who does he think he is, some kind of ghostly vigilante who leaks dust wherever he goes?'

He laughed. 'Look, don't let that corny old tape get to you. It's just one old geezer reading off a script. And another relic standing beside him doing the so-called sound-effects with a milk bottle and a coconut. And anyway, the Creeper is safely tucked away in your drawer now. He can't bother you any more.' He got up. 'I'm not allowed to stay long.' And I suddenly noticed how Mum hadn't brought up a tray of juice and biscuits as she normally did when my friends called. It made me realize how ill I must be.

'You'd better not get too close,' I said. 'I'd hate you to catch this bug.'

'Don't worry about me. And I'll look in on you again soon. I sound like your doctor, don't I?'

'Thanks for calling round.'

'I'll be back.' His voice already sounded far away as I drifted off to sleep. Once I opened my eyes and thought I heard the Creeper whispering. Only his voice was so faint I couldn't make out what he was saying. 'You're just a dream,' I murmured to myself, 'or a power surge,' and soon I was asleep again.

Next morning I felt a little better but I still didn't have much appetite. Mum changed the sheets while I sat in her and Dad's double bed.

'Right, you can hop back in,' said Mum. 'Take your time now.'

I hobbled back into my bed.

'There, does that feel nice and fresh?'

I considered. 'I think I prefer your bed, actually.'

Mum laughed, then handed me yet another glass of juice. 'By the way, I saw Amy's mum yesterday.'

I nearly spilt the juice over myself. 'Did you?' I croaked.

'Why didn't you tell me what had happened?' asked Mum.

I gripped the glass tightly, wondering if I should pretend to pass out at this point. 'I was too ashamed,' I began.

'But you've done nothing to be

ashamed of,' replied Mum indignantly. 'You've been a really good friend to Amy. You looked after her when she started here and she was such a shy, nervous girl at first. You helped her, and this is how she repays you.'

Mum sat down on my bed. 'I must say I thought it was a bit strange when Amy didn't ring up to see how you were. So you and she have had an argument. Is that right?'

I nodded.

'Do you want to tell me what the argument was about?'

I wanted to tell Mum exactly what I'd said on Thursday afternoon. It would be a relief to tell someone, to confess. Yet if Mum knew the truth she wouldn't be completely on my side as she was now.

So instead I said, 'We argued about this other girl.'

'Natalie,' interrupted Mum.

'That's right.'

'Amy's mother mentioned her. She thinks she's a bad influence.'

'So has Natalie been round Amy's house a lot?'

'I believe so, yes.'

I put the glass of juice back on the bedside table as my hand was starting to tremble. I continued, 'On Friday, before school, Amy said I should get a new best friend as she didn't want to go round with me any more and she needed to have her best-friend chain back too. Well, actually Natalie said the last bit; she didn't argue though.'

'But that's awful.' Mum was practically crying. 'Amy's mother never mentioned any of this. She said Amy wouldn't talk about why you and she weren't friends any more.'

I felt so ashamed then, as if I'd betrayed Amy for a second time, blabbing out – well, if not lies – half-truths. Yet I didn't say any of this to Mum. Instead, I lay there basking in her sympathy.

But then Mum had to go and answer the phone and all at once I felt so unhappy. For the past few days I'd tried really hard to drive all the misery and guilt I felt about Amy far away. But those feelings can't have been very far away, because they came rushing back so fast. Before Mum had even got down the stairs in fact.

Soon I was picturing Amy and Natalie sitting together at school, ringing each other up in the evenings, making plans for the weekend. It was torture but I couldn't stop myself following them.

Later Amy turned up again in a dream. She and I were arguing. Amy had discovered what I'd said about her to my mum and she was furious.

'It wasn't all lies. You have dumped me for Natalie,' I cried.

'Only because of what you said on Thursday. I still can't believe how you broke my trust in you. You did something unforgivable.'

'I know,' I agreed miserably.

'And just wait until your mum finds out the truth. She'll hate you as much as I do. I'm off to tell her now.'

'No, don't do that, please. I beg you.'

But Amy just laughed and ran off. Her feet went tap, tap, tap. I was still trying to catch up with her when I jumped awake.

It was the middle of the night. An eerie silence hung over my room like a fog. I peered around. My gaze stopped at the wardrobe.

There was that shape again. But I wouldn't be fooled this time. I knew it was my coat. Then, with a horrible thud, I remembered something: Dad had thought that coat might be giving me nightmares and had taken it downstairs.

So if it wasn't my coat . . . ?

I stared at it out of the corner of my eye. A shadow, that's all I could see. It wasn't moving. Yet I caught a glint of colour – like a spark of fire.

The Creeper.

He was here, watching me with his terrible eyes.

I tried to call out but fear had got into my throat. I just managed the tiniest, scratchiest sound you've ever heard.

Suddenly a cry tore from me. 'Dad!' Almost instantly my dad rushed in.

'It's over there,' I cried, pointing at the wardrobe.

Dad went through his pantomime of checking the room, even looking under my bed. Though I never expected it to be hiding there. The Creeper could sneak away through my window in an instant. That's why I made Dad close the window.

'Are you sure? I thought you couldn't sleep with the window closed.'

'Tonight I can.'

'Well, it feels really hot in here already.' A shudder ran through me.

Dad went on staring at me, puzzled and anxious.

Next morning Mum had a long chat with me about my nightmare or hallucination: they're a type of nightmare but with special effects. And you can have them when you're awake too.

She said we're especially prone to hallucinations when we're ill because that's when our mind starts to play tricks on us. So I'd been having hallucinations. In a way that was scary too, but at least there was a proper explanation.

Later I got out of bed to go to the loo. For a moment I paused by the wardrobe, remembering again the strange figure I'd seen – or my hallucination, as I must call it. Then I glanced at the window sill. I couldn't believe what I saw.

I bent down and stared more closely. No, it was really there. My heart charged furiously.

Along the window sill was a small trail of greyish dust.

Chapter Nine

Jack crouched down and stared at the dust like a detective studying a clue. I was sitting on the bed in my dressing gown.

I'd been waiting for him all day. I had to tell someone, and I knew my mum and dad wouldn't understand.

He looked up. 'Messy little blighter, isn't he?'

'So you think that is the Creeper's . . . ?' I hesitated.

'Calling card,' said Jack. 'I don't know.'

'It is him, Jack.' I was whispering now. 'He's been here in this room. And there's the proof. I couldn't have dreamt that, could I?'

Jack didn't answer. The only sound in the room was the rain drumming against the window. It was just four o'clock but already it was pitch dark. You couldn't see a thing outside.

'Well, say something,' I said. 'Don't just stand there like Inspector Clouseau.'

'Sssh, I'm thinking. So, on the window sill is a bit of the Creeper's body.'

I began to shiver.

'You ought to get back into bed,' he said.

'I'm not cold – just scared,' I murmured. 'I've been thinking about this all day. The Creeper's been in my room, hasn't he?'

'He might have been. I was just wondering . . .'

'Yes?'

'Well, it's only a theory.'

'Say it.'

'Just suppose your tape is haunted.'

I stared at him.

'If you like,' he went on, 'I'll take the tape away with me. Then perhaps all this tapping and dust-leaking might stop.'

'That's a good idea,' I whispered. 'I'll get you the tape now.' I went over to the dressing table. 'I put it right at the bottom here, under my . . .' I stopped. A trembling fear began in my knees. It quickly took over my whole body. I swallowed hard. 'Well, this changes everything,' I said, in a low, strangled voice.

'What do you mean?' began Jack.

I slowly pulled the tape out of the drawer. Then he saw what I saw.

I'd seen tapes unspooled before. I remember putting one in a dodgy tape recorder and at once the tape was spewed out all over the place.

But my tape had been tucked safely away in a drawer. No-one had touched it. Yet somehow it had managed to unravel all by itself.

Jack couldn't believe his eyes. 'It's impossible. But how did that . . . ?' He looked at me. 'The Creeper's escaped, hasn't he?'

Chapter Ten

Jack immediately tried to laugh off what he'd said. 'He's escaped. Now there's a corny line, used in about a zillion horror movies. No, what's happened is—'

'My tape unwound itself all on its own. I don't think so, Jack.' I got up. 'Playing the tape was like waking him up, wasn't it? And now he's unwound himself out of my tape and he's hiding in my room.'

'I don't see him.'

My voice rose. 'But he's somewhere nearby, isn't he? Just waiting to creep back inside my room when it's dark.'

From downstairs came my mum's voice: 'Everything all right?'

'Yes, fine, thanks,' I called back. Then I murmured, 'The Creeper's only hatched out in my drawer, that's all.'

'Lucy, sit down and let's be calm about this,' urged Jack. 'We've got to work out what to do next.'

I sat down on the edge of my bed. My teeth were starting to chatter. I wrapped my arms about myself, then looked at Jack expectantly.

'Now, let's say the Creeper was waiting in the tape. He's probably been stuck in there for years. Then you played the tape, and when the story finished he was able to, somehow, get out.' He paused.

'And now?'

'He's climbed out of the tape for good.'

I let out a cry of horror.

'But here's the good news: I reckon the Creeper was only trying out his powers on you as a kind of warm-up, before he goes off and scares some wrong-doers. That's how the Creeper enjoys himself, isn't it? I'm amazed he's stayed around you for so long.' He grinned. 'You haven't got any guilty secrets, have you?'

I started.

'You haven't robbed any banks, or mugged a hamster lately, have you?'

I managed to smile. But racing through my head was the thought: Yes, I *have* done something bad. I betrayed Amy. Did the Creeper know that? Was that why he was still hanging around?

Jack continued, 'The Creeper's bound to get bored of you and go after some real villains. I bet he's already decided to leave you alone.' He knelt down. 'Are you OK?'

'I do feel a bit groggy.' I climbed back into bed.

'Do you want me to get—?'

'No, I'll be fine,' I interrupted.

'You're the only one I can talk to about this, Jack. My parents wouldn't understand the significance of the dust, or even that tape. They'd think I'd put it away all mashed up like that; I know I didn't.'

'I believe you,' said Jack. 'Look, we're in this together. We'll sort out Dust-breath, have no fear. But you've got nothing to worry about.' He gave a cheeky smile. 'Face it, Lucy, you're just not the Creeper's type.'

Jack really cheered me up and I began to think he was right, too: the Creeper had just been testing out his powers on me, seeing if he could still scare people. Well, now he knew that he could he'd be off after much bigger game than me.

I felt sorry for whoever the Creeper descended on next; but relieved I was out of his sights.

I listened to the rain battering against my window. Tonight it was oddly comforting. For the Creeper's one enemy was the rain. He'd be sheltering somewhere now.

Later I remember Mum bustling in, drawing the curtains and saying: 'The rain's stopped at last, but the garden's half-flooded.' I don't recall my reply or anything else until I woke up with the prickly feeling that I was not alone.

When I opened my eyes would I see a dark figure in the corner of my room, waiting? I was too scared to look. Instead, I huddled under the sheets, my heart hammering against my ribs.

Then I heard a rustling noise as if someone were folding up a newspaper. The Creeper was moving nearer to me. I stayed buried under the sheets, terrified, and trapped.

Would the Creeper suddenly pounce on me?

The whole room seemed to be hushed and holding its breath. I closed my eyes tightly. Time passed. And then finally, I popped my nose out. The air certainly felt colder. More of my head appeared. I took a peek around, then another.

He'd definitely gone.

I clambered out of bed, put my light on and went over to the window sill.

Another trail of dust was waiting for me.

For once Jack was wrong. The Creeper hadn't gone off in search of new victims. He was still lurking around me. And suddenly I knew why: it was obvious, wasn't it?

The Creeper had already picked his next victim: me.

Chapter Eleven

I hardly slept at all that night. One question raced around my head: why was the Creeper still terrorizing me?

There was only one answer, and it came from his own dusty lips: 'The Creeper knows your guilty secret.'

Somehow, everything came back to that. It was such a horrible secret – and I couldn't keep it to myself any longer. I had to tell someone what I'd done.

I decided I'd tell Jack the whole story.

I waited impatiently for him all day. Then, just before he arrived, I closed my eyes for a minute and promptly fell asleep.

The next thing I knew was Jack's voice saying, 'Are you awake, Lucy?'

'Yes, I'm awake,' I cried. My eyes flew open.

He was leaning over me. 'Feeling any better?'

'Sort of,' I said doubtfully.

'No more visits from Dust-breath,' he went on, very bright and breezy.

'Yes, there was.'

Jack gaped at me.

'The Creeper was in my room last night. And afterwards he left his usual trademark. It's still there.' Jack darted over to the window sill. He looked down at the dust, then across at me. He was stunned. 'I know he'll be back,' I said.

Jack shook his head in puzzlement, his dark green jumper shimmering in the afternoon sunlight. 'I just don't get it.' He seemed to be speaking more to himself than me. 'Why should the Creeper still be hanging around here?'

'I think I know. I haven't told you

all the facts. There's something about me you don't know.' I reached across and had a sip of water. 'I did something very bad recently.'

'Excellent.' Jack's eyes glinted with amusement.

'No, this isn't funny. And what I'm telling you is in the strictest confidence. All right?'

Jack sat on the edge of the bed. He looked more serious than I'd ever known him. 'You can trust me, Lucy.'

I took a deep breath. 'You know I've become best friends with Amy.'

'Mmm,' he said vaguely.

'Well, Amy trusted me so much she told me something very personal. Last year Amy's dad left home to live with his new lady-friend. He was away for about six months and Amy hardly saw him. Her mum was really upset and it was a very bad time all round.

'But then her dad came home. He and Amy's mum made up and they decided to have a completely fresh start somewhere else. So they moved here where no-one else knew about their past, except me. I was honoured Amy had trusted me with this secret, and promised her I would never tell anyone else.'

Jack nodded gravely, his eyes fixed on me.

'But then Natalie came on the scene. At first she'd been quite snidey to Amy, as she is to most people.'

'I can tell you really like her,' interrupted Jack.

'Oh, she's always spreading rumours about people. I was certain she was saying things about me. And I knew she wanted to mess up my friendship with Amy.'

'So why didn't you just throw a tennis ball at her or something?'

'Typical boy's response.'

'I apologize for being a boy. Go on.'

'Lately I'd noticed Amy wasn't quite so friendly to me.'

'You should have just played it cool. She'd have come round again.'

'You're probably right, but instead I got more and more worked up. Then, on Halloween afternoon I was walking out of school with Amy when Natalie came along, completely taking over the conversation, as usual. Well, I walked off, then my dad popped up. Only he hadn't got changed properly. He still had his suit jacket on but with his hideous tracksuit bottoms.'

'All dads have got bad taste in clothes,' said Jack. 'It's compulsory.'

'I know, but Natalie started laughing at my dad. Then Amy joined in and I heard her call my dad a prat.

That did it. In a complete fury I cried, "All right, my dad dresses really badly, but at least he's never run away from home with another woman like yours, Amy." '

Jack let out a sharp breath.

'I know. I know,' I cried, lowering my head. 'I'd give anything not to have said it. Anything. And if you'd seen Amy's face: she couldn't believe what I'd done. And I couldn't either. I'd been so evil and disloyal, and to someone I really cared about too.'

'And Natalie heard all this?'

'I'm afraid she did. The only thing is, I don't think she believed me. You see, Natalie reckons I'm a liar, which I am – I'm always making up things.' My voice fell away. 'I'm so ashamed, Jack.'

There was silence for a moment. Then Jack said, 'But you didn't mean to say it. It wasn't as if you'd planned it. You just blurted something out on the spur of the moment.'

'I shouldn't have said it at all,' I whispered. 'I broke Amy's trust in me – and I hurt her so badly. If only I could unsay it. But I can't. And when I tried to apologize to Amy she blanked me out and said she didn't want to know me any more. I haven't spoken to her since.'

Jack considered. 'There's still one thing I don't understand. What's this got to do with the Creeper?'

'I've just explained.'

'You got mad and said something you shouldn't and upset a good friend. But you're not really a bad person. I mean, you wouldn't burn someone in a barn just to get their money, would you?'

'No, of course not.' I was shocked at the very idea.

'I still don't get it,' muttered Jack. 'Unless . . .'

'Yes?'

'Well, the Creeper's been locked in this tape for a long time, hasn't he? So when he finally gets out it's as if he hasn't eaten for ages. He's starving hungry for something, anything. Now, usually he wouldn't bother with you, but he's picked up on your guilt and because he hasn't been out much lately he's made a home here.'

'That really cheers me up.'

'But don't you see?' cried Jack. 'The Creeper doesn't know what you've done wrong, but maybe he can smell the guilt on you like a perfume. And then – well, he's like a bee around a honey pot, isn't he? And as long as you sit here feeling guilty the Creeper will hang around too. Am I making sense?'

'Yes, you are,' I said slowly. 'So if I stop feeling guilty . . .'

'The Creeper will vanish away on to a more deserving victim.'

Jack rubbed his hands together. 'Well, that's your problem solved.'

'Except for one thing – how can I stop feeling guilty? I mean, I let my best friend down.'

'But you didn't mean . . .'

'That doesn't help, Jack.'

He considered. 'I bet if you rang Amy you'd be friends again in no time.'

'Do you think so?'

'Definitely. When you saw her before her anger was still fresh. Now she's had time to get over it. Plus, she knows you've been ill, so you can play on her sympathy too. Cough a lot when you're asking her to forgive you.'

'You're not taking this very seriously, are you?'

'Yes I am, but come on, we all say things we don't mean. Nasty things too, and often they're to the people we like the most. I've never quite figured out why, but it's a known fact. And Amy won't want to lose your friendship over one stupid comment. She's probably sitting at home now wondering why you haven't called.'

'She's forgotten all about me. She just wants to be with Natalie now.'

'I don't think so, but I'm only a boy, so what do I know.'

'Exactly.'

We smiled at each other.

'You can sort it out,' he said, 'and get rid of the Creeper too. A double whammy.' He walked over to the door, then whispered, 'Go on, ring her now.'

Jack made it all seem really simple. One phone call, one apology and then – well, if Amy and I weren't best friends, at least we'd be talking again.

And I'd have defeated the Creeper too.

I ran through in my mind what I was going to say to Amy. I felt sick with nerves. But this was something I had to do.

I asked Mum if I could borrow her mobile phone. She looked surprised. I think she was about to ask me who

I wanted to ring up. But in the end she thought better of it and said, 'Yes, of course, love.'

I sat up in bed, the mobile phone in my hand. I didn't need to look up Amy's number. I'd rung it so many times in the past I knew it by heart – 837247.

It was ringing. My heart began to beat as if in accompaniment. I wondered if her mum would answer. That was all right, her mum liked me. But it was Amy's voice I heard. She recited their number.

I began to speak. Already I sounded out of breath. 'Hi, Amy, it's Lucy. I just thought I'd ring up to say how sorry I am about everything and see how you are. I'm still in bed with this flu bug, worse luck. But I'm feeling a bit better. So how are you?'

A tiny click was my only answer. It seemed to pierce right through me. I couldn't believe it. I didn't put the phone down for ages; I sat listening to the phone making that strange whirring noise.

Then I saw Mum standing, watching me. I snapped the phone down. 'She was out.'

'Oh, right, maybe try again later,' said Mum. But I knew from her tone that she didn't believe me. 'Perhaps it's best you concentrate on getting well for now.'

But how could I? What a complete mess. Outside it was starting to get dark. And the Creeper was out there, waiting. What could I do?

With Amy not even speaking to me I was stuck. Maybe I'd never be able to get rid of the Creeper.

And then it came to me: a really wild idea.

Chapter Twelve

My idea was actually quite simple.

The Creeper had escaped out of a story and could never go back to it because the tape was all mangled up. But maybe, just maybe, he could be lured into another one: a new story.

I thought about the plan for a long time. I decided to dictate my tale on to a tape. Mum found a blank tape downstairs for me. I told her I was putting down some ideas for a project at school. I heard her whispering to Dad that this was a good sign.

I tried to tell my story in the same style as the old one so that the Creeper would feel at home. And when I began I hadn't meant to use any real names. Honestly!

Here's how my version started:

The Creeper, moving as silently as any shadow, peered through windows seeing the good and bad deeds people did. The Creeper had been cruelly wronged once. Now he took revenge on all wrong-doers.

That night he approached his first victim. She lived in a very big house with three bathrooms – the last house down Aysley Avenue. She had everything money could buy. She was so fortunate, yet she'd caused such harm to other innocent people.

I paused. Almost without realizing it I was describing Natalie. I should stop. But I couldn't. So I went on:

The Creeper peered through the window, he had never seen such an enormous bedroom. Then he tapped solemnly on the window.

Natalie sprang up in bed clutching her deluxe doll. But then she decided it must be the wind. She snuggled down in her vast bed again. Suddenly she began to feel very hot. She slowly opened her eyes, then screamed in terror. A strange, shadowy figure stood in front of her. She screamed again.

But no-one heard either of her screams – one of the disadvantages of living in a mansion.

'Who are you?' she cried.

'I am the Creeper. I know your guilty secret.'

'What guilty secret?' she spluttered.

'You have so much, yet you still do nasty things. Lucy only had one friend, Amy. But you plotted to take Amy away from her.'

'No, no,' she spluttered again.

'The Creeper sees everything.'

'Please listen. I'll give you anything.'

But the Creeper grew weary of her. He raised his ugly, misshapen claw of *a hand. One final scream and Natalie's mouth was stilled for ever. She lay there locked in a look of terror. 'I do not think I shall unfreeze you,' said the Creeper. 'I'd be helping the world if you never spoke again.'*

I paused. I should have stopped the story there. Instead, I blinked away angry tears and said:

The Creeper had one more call to make. This was to a much smaller house in Gartree Drive, the one on the corner. A girl lay sleeping soundly. She never heard the Creeper tap softly on her window. She never saw him creep through the window, which was open very slightly.

Suddenly she felt very hot, just as if she was burning up. Then she saw a pair of orange eyes staring at her.

'Who . . . ?' was all she could gasp.

'I am the Creeper. I see everything, Amy. I know how you have let your friend, Lucy, down. You dropped her when Natalie—'

'No, I didn't,' she cried. 'She betrayed me.'

'And you never gave her a chance to

explain. Now she lies ill and you haven't once phoned to see how she is. And today when Lucy called you to apologize, what did you do? Slam the phone down on her. What kind of friend are you?'

Before she could reply the Creeper had raised his gruesome hand. 'Mercy,' she gasped.

'What mercy did you show your friend when she called you today?' said the Creeper. 'Answer me that.'

But Amy couldn't answer anyone now. She was too petrified.

I stopped there. I couldn't bring myself to have Amy frozen for ever. I lay back, exhausted. But now came the tricky part of my plan.

The dangerous part.

How was I going to coax the Creeper into my tape? It was a bit like trying to return a genie to its bottle.

I ran the plan over and over in my mind. I mustn't sleep tonight. Instead, I must lie waiting for the Creeper to appear. Then I'd switch on the story. The Creeper would be so fascinated he'd wander inside the tape, and then I'd have caught him. As soon as that happened I'd yank the tape off immediately and put it back in its proper case for ever. After which the Creeper would never be able to torment me, or anyone else, again.

He'd stay imprisoned in my tape for – well, for as long as I lived anyway.

As it got darker I became more and more nervous. I wished Jack were here. Still, I told myself if I succeeded Jack would be extremely impressed.

But what if I didn't succeed? What if the whole scheme went wrong? I had no way of defending myself.

Then I remembered the Creeper's one enemy.

Later, when Mum came in I told her how thirsty I got at night: could

she bring me a jug, rather than just
a glass of water? Then I kept edging
the jug of water nearer to me. Right
next to it was the tape recorder. I was
armed and ready. I lay back and
waited.

I heard Mum come lightly upstairs.
Dad trudged up a bit later. Then I
listened to the house creak and
wheeze as the heating was switched
off and it cooled down for the night.
My radiator started its nightly
gurgling – or that's exactly what it
sounded like. When I was younger I
used to hate that noise; now I almost
liked it.

Outside a cat let out a yowl of
alarm. Had it caught a glimpse of the
Creeper? I lay trembling with excitement and fear. I felt like a hunter
waiting by a trap.

After a while I grew drowsy. But I kept shaking myself awake. There was nothing to hear, then there was. Three faint tapping noises on the window. I had left my window slightly ajar. Was the Creeper inside yet?

My breathing became fast. But I had to stay calm, I told myself. If my plan worked, in a few moments the Creeper would be locked away, never to be released again.

As always, my bedroom was full of shadows and they acted as excellent camouflage for the Creeper. It was hard to tell if he was prowling about my room or not.

But I decided he must be. It just took a couple of seconds to press down the play button on my tape recorder. Then I buried my head beneath my pillow. I didn't want to see the Creeper. I just wanted him to vanish away into that story.

I'd kept the volume down low so that my mum and dad wouldn't come rushing in. But it still felt strange hearing myself whispering away in the middle of the night. I was saying: *The Creeper had one more call to make. This was to a much smaller house in Gartree Drive, the one on the corner.* Then I realized I hadn't run the tape back far enough. I was starting in the middle of the tape, with the story about Amy.

Soon afterwards the story finished. Should I rewind it? Or had that been enough? Was the Creeper in my tape now? I sat up looking about very cautiously. I couldn't see anything, and my bedroom certainly didn't feel particularly hot. It seemed as if the Creeper had gone.

A few lines of a story and the Creeper just slipped away. Or had he?

Then my mind made an awful leap: what if the Creeper really had gone, not into my tape, but off to Amy's house? It was possible, wasn't it? I'd even given him Amy's address.

I lay there picturing Amy suddenly awoken by the Creeper. She'd be terrified, even more scared than me.

Amy likes horror films, but she watches them through her fingers. She told me once she could never watch a horror film on her own.

And I've just sent her a real horror story, one that would terrify the wits out of her. Oh Amy, what have I done? I don't deserve to have a friend like you if this is how I treat you.

I sat up in bed, my head throbbing. I almost wanted the Creeper to be here now. Anything would be better than thinking he was at Amy's house.

And I'd sent him there too.

Should I ring Amy and warn her to keep all her windows bolted? But what could I tell her? This evil character on a tape has escaped, and I think he's on his way to your house.

Besides, the Creeper might be

there by now. I let out a cry of frustration.

And then I heard a rustling noise like leaves shaking on a tree.

I was not alone.

Chapter Thirteen

Something stirred by my wardrobe. It was little more than a small silhouette at first. But then he came gliding towards me as lightly and easily as a ghost.

I could make out the features on his face, but even up close they looked as if they'd been lightly sketched on. They didn't seem quite real – except for his eyes. They glowed with an intensity I had never seen before. And flashes of blue, green and red darted in and out of the Creeper's eyes too.

I was transfixed.

I couldn't look away from his stare.

His eyes held me. I felt the hairs prickle on my head. I had never been more terrified.

He drew nearer. With him came the smell of burning fires. But he looked as solid as the wardrobe behind him.

'The Creeper saw what you did,' he whispered. Tiny flecks of dust shot over my bed as he spoke.

I found myself gabbling. 'Do you mean the story I made up? Yes, I'm sorry, it wasn't very long. And those names I used, they do belong to real people, but don't visit them, please. They're not . . . well, I'm the guilty one. But you know that. Jack said you can smell my guilt, like perfume.' I paused and took a long, choking breath. Sweat was dripping off my forehead. 'What do you want with me?' I croaked.

There was no reply at first. But the

Creeper's eyes blazed furiously. Then he hissed softly, like a fire sizzling, 'The Creeper is very angry.'

A wave of terror swept through me. For days he'd been stalking me, now he was about to pounce. And I was utterly defenceless, like an animal caught in the open.

Then I remembered.

But I had to act fast. I fumbled for the handle of the jug and then hurled as much water as I could in the Creeper's direction. Some of it landed on the bed but enough of it reached him.

I saw his eyes open wide with astonishment: he obviously hadn't expected any attack at all. Then came this hissing noise like water on a hot plate, followed by a great shower of sparks. The sparks fell away into the darkness and so did the Creeper. Before my eyes he dwindled away into oblivion.

He gave one tiny piteous squeal as if he were an animal caught in a dreadful trap. And then he was no more.

I sat up. I had destroyed the Creeper. But I didn't feel the least bit triumphant. Instead, I thought of that squealing noise. Yet he'd left me no choice. I was only defending myself.

I sat on the edge of my bed, my heart thumping away. And then, out of the corner of my eye, I saw on the carpet a tiny glimmer of light. I stared at it. The light started to move. It hopped around my carpet like a bird trying to fly.

Suddenly it soared upwards and all these pieces of dust began to fly into the air. The dust swirled round and round, like a kind of whirlwind. My lampshade swung wildly. My curtains shook.

I was dizzy with fear and the scorching heat. It was so hot I wouldn't have been surprised if my wallpaper had caught fire. The heat on my skin seemed to be sucking my energy away.

All I could do was sit there and watch the water on my carpet turn to steam, and then see . . . The Creeper's legs were there first, all by themselves. They stood dead still, waiting. Then quickly, expertly, the dust reformed itself into a body. And finally, that face, which belonged only in nightmares, loomed over me once more.

I shrank back in bed. I could hear the Creeper hissing to himself. He sounded like a swarm of angry bees. And then those eyes were fixed upon me once more.

I hadn't destroyed him at all. The water had only stunned him. But as soon as the dust had dried he was back, and angrier than ever. There was only one thing left to do: make a run for it. But this time the Creeper anticipated me.

Up to now I'd scarcely noticed his undead hand, because my attention had been fixed on those eyes and he'd tucked that hand across his stomach so it was partly hidden. But with lightning swiftness the Creeper raised his hand in front of me.

It was like a great claw, but it could have been a thousand years old. For it was all shrivelled like a squeezed orange. The fingernails weren't black, as in the picture I'd seen. They were yellowy brown. And although there had been blood on the drawing, this was quite different.

For the blood which ran down the Creeper's hand now shone and glistened. It looked fresh.

The Creeper drew his hand out as if it were a sword. But actually it was much deadlier. For straight away I felt a blast of hot air run down my arms. Before I could react, more heat came shooting up my spine. And the heat was like a great, heavy weight pressing down on me.

'Whaa . . .' It took every ounce of strength to move my lips. I couldn't make any sense come out of them.

And then I couldn't move at all. It was as if my whole body was held in a

vice. I was completely in the Creeper's power.

His eyes were scorchingly angry. His hand moved closer to me. I wasn't able to even shut my eyes. I could only gape up mutely at this monster.

To my great surprise his hand stretched away from me and towards the tape recorder. He let out a great cry, which again sounded like an animal in terrible pain. Then he picked the tape up and threw it with great fury across the room.

'You make fun of the Creeper,' he hissed. He pushed his face closer. Musty air came with him. I attempted to shake my head but my whole body was caught in a grip of iron. I couldn't move a muscle.

His eyes glared into mine. 'The Creeper wants another story.' He spat flakes of dust on to my head, and he sounded not only angry, but humiliated.

Then he floated away from me.

I glimpsed him standing over by the wardrobe. Next I saw the curtains begin to stir as if being moved by a gentle breeze. Suddenly cold air seemed to come rushing back into the room. The temperature dropped, and I could move my body again.

It was as if a terrible weight had rolled off me. My arms and legs felt a bit stiff but that was all. I was gasping with relief. I'd feared the Creeper was going to leave me in the same state as his other victims.

But he hadn't finished with me either.

He'd said, '*The Creeper wants another story.*'

And I knew he'd be back for it.

Chapter Fourteen

The shrill ring of the telephone woke me up. I peered at my watch. It was only half past seven. Who would be calling so early? I heard Dad's voice but couldn't make out what he was saying. He didn't speak for long.

A few moments later my door slowly opened. Mum's head peered around. 'That phone woke you, didn't it?'

'Who was it?'

'Someone wanting to know how you were.'

I was stunned. 'Who?'

'A girl. She didn't give her name. She rang off when she heard you were getting better. Your dad thought it might have been Amy.'

'Amy,' I repeated. But why should she suddenly ring up to see how I was? She couldn't be bothered to even say 'hello' last night.

Of course, it might have been Natalie ringing to see if I'd popped my clogs yet. Or maybe it was someone from my form. But why call so early?

'Did she ask to speak to me?'

'I don't think so,' replied Mum. 'But then she probably thought you would still be asleep. Still, at least you know someone's thinking about you, which is nice, isn't it?'

She drew back the curtains. 'All this dust,' she muttered, brushing the window sill with her hands.

'You see it too?' I burst out.

'Of course I do.' Mum gave me a puzzled look. 'I just wonder where it all comes from.'

I could have told Mum. But I knew she'd never believe me. She'd just start talking about hallucinations again. Mum picked up the water jug.

'You were thirsty last night, weren't you?'

Last night seemed far away now. And the Creeper: he would probably be sleeping now. I wondered if he slept standing up like some birds do. Yet he'd always have one eye open, alert for any danger. Not that the Creeper had much to fear from anyone – he was practically indestructible.

And tonight he would be back here for 'another story'. I should be thinking of one. I wrote down a few ideas but tore them all up. How did I know what kind of story the Creeper wanted?

I glanced around me: I felt as if I'd been cooped up in this room for weeks. Now even the air felt stale and used up. I had to get out of here for a bit.

Mum took my temperature. It had gone down but she thought I needed another day in bed. Yet I kept on pleading with her. And in the end, very reluctantly, Mum agreed I could sit downstairs for a little while in the afternoon.

At three o'clock I got dressed. Who'd have thought going downstairs could be so exciting? I felt like a prisoner out on parole.

I walked around every room downstairs, then I sank onto the cream sofa. Mum lit the fire even though the weather had brightened up outside. And I lay watching afternoon television, waiting for Jack.

Mum was doing an interview on the phone when the doorbell rang.

Jack.

I sat up expectantly. I had so much to tell him. And if anyone knew what I should do next it would be him.

But instead my mum came in and said, in this strange voice, 'You've got a visitor, Lucy.'

And standing there was Amy.

Before she left Mum said, 'This is Lucy's first day out of bed so she's got to take it very easy.' There was a warning tone in Mum's voice, as if to say, 'Don't you dare upset her now.'

I couldn't believe Amy was here. I was totally shocked. 'Hello,' I said softly.

'Hello.' She was standing right by the door. Anyone watching us would have thought we were strangers meeting for the first time. I felt so shy and embarrassed.

'I can only stay for a minute,' went on Amy, in this tiny, expressionless voice. 'My mum's waiting outside.'

'Oh right,' I murmured.

'I just came round to see how you are.' She was staring intently at the carpet as if the answer was there.

'Oh, I'm feeling better now. It's just so good to be out of bed. I feel as if I've been stuck up there for months.' I gave a half-laugh.

But Amy just nodded gravely and said, 'Right, that's all I wanted to know. I'm glad you're getting better.'

She turned to go.

'So has someone been saying I'm really ill? Has Natalie been spreading rumours about me again?' My voice had gone all high-pitched.

'It's nothing to do with Natalie.' She sounded irritated.

'It was you who rang up this morning, wasn't it?'

'Yes, it was.' Her face reddened.

I realized with a shock how much I'd missed Amy. I was still missing her. The old Amy. My true friend.

She turned to go again, then

suddenly whirled round. 'I'll tell you why I rang this morning. Last night I had a nightmare about you.'

'Oh,' I murmured, not sure how to react.

'It was really horrible. You were lying in bed when this figure appeared out of nowhere. It was like a shadow but with the most evil eyes and a claw for a hand that was all burnt.' Amy must have seen me start forward because she said, 'Sorry, I didn't mean to upset you.'

I could only gape at her at first. It was totally weird and uncanny. Amy had never seen the Creeper, yet she'd described him perfectly from her nightmare. How was this possible?

'No, you haven't upset me,' I said at last. 'Go on.'

'Well, he looked a bit like the Grim Reaper, you know, Death. And I thought, Why is the Grim Reaper hunched over Lucy like that, as if she's his next victim?' Her voice fell. 'When I woke up I thought maybe that dream was a premonition. I wanted to go downstairs and ring you

271

right then to check you were all right. But it was the middle of the night so I couldn't . . . but next morning – I mean, my mum thought I was mad – I had to call.'

My stomach tightened. Even though Amy wasn't my friend any more she still couldn't help sensing when I was in danger. She'd even seen the Creeper. And she cared enough to call round.

I knew what I had to say. 'Look, Amy, I'm truly, truly, sorry.'

She lowered her face.

'I know I shouldn't have—'

'No, you shouldn't,' she interrupted fiercely. 'I trusted you.'

'I know.'

'I told you that in complete confidence. You shouldn't have said anything – and the way you just . . .'

'I shocked myself. I was incredibly spiteful but at least Natalie doesn't believe what I said was true.'

'She did at first. But I managed to persuade her it was another of your fairy stories.'

'Well, that's something,' I said

softly. 'Natalie always bugs me. You know that. So when you ganged up with her and started making fun of my dad and those clothes he was wearing . . .'

'I never did any such thing.' Amy's voice rose indignantly.

'You did, Amy. I heard you.'

'No, you didn't. I was telling Natalie what my dad wears when he's decorating. I said he looks a right prat. That's what we were laughing about. I swear.'

I didn't know what to say. I just swallowed hard. This whole, terrible falling-out had been over nothing. My eyes began to smart.

I noticed Amy had sat down on the edge of the chair opposite me. She said, 'I didn't mean to put the phone down on you yesterday. You just took me by surprise.' Before I could reply Amy went on, 'I know you've helped me a lot. But you don't own me. I'll be friends with whoever I choose. And if Natalie invites me round to her house . . . why shouldn't I go?'

'Why shouldn't you?' I said quietly. 'So what's it like there? Has she really got three bathrooms?'

'Oh yes. It's a huge house, but there's a funny atmosphere. Natalie's got this little sister who's just completely spoilt. She called me cow-face.'

'How rude.'

'Natalie and her mum just laughed. And do you know what we had for our tea? Macaroni cheese. It was disgusting. It looked just like someone had been sick all over my plate.'

I began to laugh. 'So did you eat any of it?'

'Well, I closed my eyes and held my nose, but I still felt as if I was eating vomit.'

We were both laughing now.

Then Amy said unexpectedly, 'I never really liked Natalie very much, you know.'

I gazed at her in surprise.

'She was so nasty when I started, always making fun of me. I hated her for that, yet I wanted to be in with her too. Do you know what I mean?'

'I think so, yes.'

'So then when she wanted to be friends with me and was trailing after me all the time . . . well, I couldn't believe it. It was very flattering. But . . .'

Before she could say anything else the door opened, making us both jump. 'Amy, what's your mum doing sitting out there in the car?'

'Well, I was only going to be a minute,' said Amy.

'Nonsense,' said Mum. She insisted Amy's mum come inside for a cup of tea. Our two mums had always got on well. Soon they were chatting away in the kitchen while Amy started filling me in on what I'd missed at school.

At that moment I didn't care what I'd missed at school. I just wanted to know if Amy had forgiven me. I thought she had. But I'd have liked her to say it. Still, with our mums flying in and out we couldn't really talk about such important matters. So I just whispered, 'I'm really glad you came round today.'

Suddenly I remembered about Jack. Every day he'd come round at the same time. Today he was late. I wondered where he was. All at once he was in the doorway.

He went over and stood in front of the mantelpiece where the ornaments and family photographs – including one ghastly snap of me – lived. Jack immediately glanced at that photo. It was taken of me when I was about two. And I look as if I've got a disease. I'm also practically bald. But my parents won't take it down. Jack burst out laughing at it. Amy had her back to him.

'Amy,' I raised my hand, pointing towards the mantelpiece – and Jack.

Amy turned round and her face broke into a big smile. I thought that was a bit odd.

So I said rather formally, 'May I introduce . . .'

She grinned at me. 'You've forgotten, haven't you?'

'Forgotten?' I faltered.

'I know all your embarrassing secrets,' she said.

I gazed at her in bewilderment. I couldn't believe she was being so rude, calling Jack an embarrassing secret. But Jack didn't seem to care. He was still laughing.

Amy strode over to Jack. But instead of saying 'hello' she grabbed the ghastly photograph. 'I know all about this,' she said. 'You showed it to me ages ago. You must remember.'

I could only gape at her. Why was she wittering on about that picture when Jack was standing right beside her?

Amy seemed to be doing her best to ignore him. But then she did something truly amazing: still with the picture in her hand she turned and walked straight through Jack.

Chapter Fifteen

I thought I must be dreaming. My breath came in heavy gasps.

'Lucy, are you all right?' Amy was staring anxiously at me.

I struggled to reply.

'You're not, are you?' She gave my arm a little pat, then rushed off to get Mum.

I looked up. Jack was still standing by the mantelpiece. He winked at me. He seemed highly amused by the whole thing. But I couldn't smile. For I'd just realized something incredible.

Everyone else was flapping around me. I was helped upstairs despite my

protests that I was 'all right, really'.

Amy and her mum left shortly afterwards while Mum tut-tutted at me. 'I knew you were overdoing it. I told you to wait until tomorrow. You weren't ready. Now you must have a good rest.'

I snuggled down in bed feeling a bit silly and self-conscious. Mum wasn't aware we were being watched by a figure who had followed us upstairs and was now sprawled out on my swing chair.

Mum closed the door and I blurted out, 'You – you're not real, are you?'

Jack sighed. 'I am realistically challenged – yes.' Then he added, 'But you should know.'

'I know I should. I mean, I do.' I stopped. Already I was getting muddled. 'It's just . . .'

'Yes?'

'These past days so much has gone wrong, but I thought at least you . . .' I hesitated.

'Spit it out.'

'I thought we were in this together.'

'We are. I'm your friend – your wish-friend.'

I smiled. 'My wish-friend. I like that.'

'And you and I go back a long way.'

'I know. It was ages ago when I first saw you. I was feeling dead lonely and suddenly, there you were. You've always cheered me up.'

Jack gave a little bow. 'I used to enjoy it when you tried out your stories on me, the ones you made up about your exciting weekends.'

'And if you liked them I'd tell the stories on Monday at school. You were really helpful. And then when Benji died you came round every night for weeks.'

'That's what a wish-friend is for. We know when to appear – and disappear. As soon as Amy came on the scene I realized it was goodbye, Jack.

Well, until Halloween night when you were so miserable you called me back.'

'I can't tell you how pleased I was to see you that night in your Dracula costume.'

Jack nodded approvingly. 'Yes, the costume was a good touch.'

'But these past days, what with me getting ill . . .' I lay back on my pillow. 'I've believed in you completely. You've seemed as real as my mum and dad – as anyone.'

'Well that's the biggest compliment you could have paid me. Cheers for that.' Then he added, 'Actually, I've felt different too, as if I weren't just imaginary, but I really did have a life of my own.'

I blinked. 'But there's something different about you today. You keep going in and out of focus. Why is that?'

Jack, who always had an answer for everything, fell unexpectedly silent. His smile dropped away. He shifted uncomfortably. Then he said abruptly, 'Look, I want to know about Dust-breath. Did he call last night?'

'He certainly did.'

'Well, come on, spill it.' He settled himself down and I recounted everything that had happened last night.

Jack listened intently, never interrupting, not even when I told him I'd put Natalie and Amy into the Creeper's story.

Then I told how the Creeper had pulled the tape out of the recorder.

'Well, he obviously didn't like that story,' said Jack. 'And I can't say I blame him. To be honest, it was pretty nasty . . . and as your wish-friend I'm allowed to say things like that.'

'You're right, too,' I mumbled quietly. I went on to say how Amy had seen the Creeper as well.

Jack let out a whistle of amazement. 'So you could say the Creeper brought you and Amy together.'

'I hadn't thought of that.'

'Well, you had, but through me,' said Jack. 'I'll tell you something else. At least you know the Creeper wants to go.'

I looked puzzled.

'If he didn't he wouldn't have asked you for another story, would he?'

'He didn't ask, he demanded.'

'Whatever, the Creeper's keen to get away into a story he likes.'

'But how on earth do I know what that is?'

'Oh, come on, Lucy.' Jack banged the arm of the chair. 'Exercise those six brain cells of yours. What have you and the Creeper got in common, apart from bad breath and a terrible temper?'

'Thanks for that.'

'You're welcome.'

I considered for a moment. 'We both love dogs and have been parted from them.'

'Exactly. But you can reunite the Creeper with Rusty, can't you?'

'I suppose I can. And you think that's what I should write the new story about?'

'Well, you could have the Creeper taking a nice, relaxing bath, but I don't think he'll go for that, do you?'

'You're getting awfully sarky all of a sudden.' I let out a cry.

'Sssh,' said Jack, 'or you'll bring your mum back.'

'I'm sorry – but you've gone all hazy around the edges. Jack, what's happening?'

Again he looked uneasy, as if I'd brought up a very touchy subject. 'It's your fault,' he said at last.

'Mine?'

'You don't need me any more.'

'Yes I do.'

'No, my time is nearly up. That's why I'm fading.'

'What about the Creeper tonight?'

'Tell the story as I suggested and then play it for the Creeper. If he likes it you'll be fine.'

'And if he doesn't?'

'Have that jug of water ready. That'll give you time to leg it out of your bedroom before he comes together again. And don't forget, you can always conjure me up. Twenty-four-hour emergency service.'

Jack shimmered to his feet. 'I would like to know how it all turns out with Dust-breath, so try and bring me back one more time, won't you?'

'Oh Jack, of course I will.'

'Well, you'd better get working on your new Creeper story.'

'Yes, sir.'

'Cheers for now . . . take care.'

And then he was gone. My wish-friend. I tried to bring him back. But I couldn't. The harder I tried, the more impossible it seemed.

It was as if I could only summon

him up when I really needed him.

So then I turned to the Creeper's story. I planned it out in my head, then dictated the story on to the tape, wiping out last night's effort first. I also remembered to rewind the tape back to the start this time.

As it grew darker I became more and more uneasy. I dreaded another encounter with the Creeper. Still, I told myself I had that jug of water. And there was Jack. If I were in trouble I was certain I could bring him back in an instant.

And two heads were always better than one – even if one of them was imaginary.

Later I fell into an uneasy sleep. When I woke up it was very dark. Sweat was running down my face. I was baking hot.

I looked up and saw that I was not alone.

A pair of orange eyes were glaring down at me.

Chapter Sixteen

The Creeper was standing beside my bed, his eyes fixed on me.

'A new story,' he said. His voice was so hoarse I could hardly hear it, but that might have been because my heart was beating so loudly.

The waves of heat he gave off were overpowering. It was like being right next to a furnace.

'I have a new story. Shall I play it for you?' I whispered.

He didn't answer, but his eyes never left me.

I stretched across and switched the tape recorder on. 'I hope you like it,' I croaked. It was difficult to speak.

The heat seemed to be clogging up my throat.

Then I heard myself on the tape saying:

Winter was drawing on and the Creeper grew weary of spying on other people. He still watched out for any sign of wrong-doing, and was quick to punish the offenders. But he was lonely.

One night he was out on his rounds when he heard this dog howling: a terrible cry of pain. The Creeper had to follow the sound. The nearer he got the more melancholy was the dog's cry. He hurried on. Then, with a jolt of horror, he recognized the dog as his own: Rusty.

Rusty was sitting by her master's grave, her face upturned to the sky. When she spotted the Creeper she bounced around him with joy. But the dog was painfully thin.

'What's the matter, Rusty, haven't your new owners been feeding you?'

But he knew they had: they were good, kindly people. Rather, it was that Rusty could not eat, could not do anything but pine for her master.

The Creeper put out a hand to the dog. Her excitement was so keen the Creeper laughed, a dry, creaky laugh. 'You don't hide from me, do you, Rusty?' he said.

Later a big storm blew up. The Creeper and Rusty took shelter in the woods. So did one of the villagers. Thunder crackled away, and then lightning flashed so bright that for an instant it lit up the Creeper.

The villager was so shocked at this sight he had to lean against the tree for support. He'd heard tales about the monster made of fire who haunted wrong-doers. This villager had a guilty secret. Would the Creeper come looking for him one night? This monster had to be destroyed. But how? Then an idea formed in his head. He went squelching off in the rain.

Dawn came, the rain stopped and the Creeper was still out in the open with his dog. In the misty light he could be seen quite easily. He was so concerned about Rusty he didn't realize the villagers were trailing him.

They advanced, each armed with a bucket of water. Then, at a signal from the villager who had devised the plan, they fired on the Creeper.

From all sides came a bombardment of water. The Creeper began to sizzle and shake, scattering his dust in all directions. Rusty gave a great howl of sadness and charged towards the villagers, barking furiously.

The Creeper dwindled away into hundreds of pieces of dust. The villagers let out a great cheer. They had destroyed the monster. They rushed off to tell the rest of the village.

Rusty was beside herself with grief. She didn't notice the dust stir as it began to dry.

When Rusty looked up again the Creeper was fully restored and thirsting for revenge.

'The Creeper sees. The Creeper knows,' he hissed. 'Come on.'

But then this boy, no more than eight or nine, ran up to the Creeper and Rusty. He patted Rusty and then stared right at the Creeper, not afraid at all. 'Everyone has been so cruel to you,' he said. 'But there's a little hut, deep in the forest.' He pointed. 'You'll be safe there.'

The Creeper stared at the boy suspiciously.

'You can rest in that hut for as long as you want,' said the boy. 'I'll come and see you later.'

The boy pointed again. Rusty sensed the boy could be trusted and began to set off. But the Creeper turned towards the village. 'I must punish them.'

Rusty barked frantically at her

master, urging him to follow her instead.

The Creeper didn't know what to do. He wanted to punish the villagers, yet he feared if he didn't follow Rusty he might never see her again.

Rusty looked at her master imploringly.

But did the Creeper go with her? Well, he certainly seems to have vanished. Some villagers claim the Creeper is still close by, hiding, waiting to strike once more. Perhaps that is true.

Or perhaps the Creeper did go after Rusty, and is now living peacefully, deep in the forest.

'The End,' I announced on the tape. Then I whispered, 'If you don't like it I can write another one for you tomorrow.'

The Creeper didn't answer. He stood still, horribly still. Was he waiting for more?

It was an awful moment, especially as I didn't dare look at the Creeper. 'It's finished now,' I repeated softly. I could have been speaking to a frightened child. Very slowly, so as not to alarm him, I reached out and switched off the tape recorder.

Then, with a movement so quick it was invisible, the Creeper's undead hand shot towards mine. There was no time to try and do anything. I was trapped.

I made a choking sound. I was sure my heart had stopped.

And then the strangest thing happened.

A rush of heat began to play around my arm and I felt a hand – the Creeper's hand – rest in mine. It was scorching hot but as light as a leaf. It stayed there just for a moment.

The next thing I knew, this thin, grey smoke had curled up in front of me. It made me cough slightly. But the smoke didn't seem to go anywhere. It just disappeared. Cold air rushed back into my room and there was a whirring noise which took me a couple of seconds to identify.

All by itself my tape recorder was rewinding at a furious rate. Finally it

stopped. Very cautiously I removed the tape. Wisps of smoke came off it. It was still hot as if it had just come out of an oven.

Gradually it cooled down, and then all that was left of the Creeper were the tiny pieces of dust scattered over my bed.

Chapter Seventeen

I suddenly felt exhausted. To my surprise I fell asleep almost at once. When I woke up I could hear Mum and Dad downstairs. I lay there thinking about the Creeper. I longed to tell Jack what had happened. So I tried to call him up.

He appeared quite easily but he was very fuzzy, and then I gasped. I'd just noticed his feet. They were floating some way above the carpet.

Jack raised his hand as if to say, Don't even ask, and demanded, 'Well, come on, tell me everything.'

So I rattled off my story. When I told him how the Creeper's hand stole into mine, Jack declared, 'You know what he was doing, don't you? He was shaking you by the hand. He was thanking you for giving him a good ending.'

'Well, he'd waited long enough for one, hadn't he?'

'You sound as if you quite like old Dust-breath now.'

'I suppose I do,' I said, surprised at my own reply. 'Some really bad things happened to him and . . . and he only acted like a monster because he was so miserable. And when you're really, really unhappy you do things you wouldn't normally do . . . mean, nasty things.'

'I'll take your word for it. Anyway, what have you done with the tape?'

I reached out. 'It's still here on my bedside table.'

Jack was shocked. 'But anyone could play it and then the Creeper could jump out again. Maybe he has to pop out of the story if the tape is played.'

'Oh, he wouldn't like that.'

'Well, do something then.'

'All right. I'll write a message on the label.'

'Make it really dramatic,' urged Jack.

So I wrote: 'DANGER – DO NOT PLAY THIS TAPE UNDER ANY CIRCUMSTANCES. YOU HAVE BEEN WARNED,' and then put it inside its box.

'Now where are you going to put it?' he asked.

'I thought I'd hide it in the jewellery box my nan bought me for my birthday. There's a little compartment at the bottom that you can lock ...'

I stopped. My bedroom door slowly opened. Mum was looking anxiously at me. 'Oh Lucy, I thought I heard you ...'

'I was working out a new story, Mum.'

Jack made a face, but Mum looked impressed. She asked me how I was feeling and then I noticed she had an envelope in her hand.

'Has someone written me a letter?'

'They have. This was delivered by hand just a few minutes ago.'

Mum hovered while I opened the letter. Out of the envelope fell a friendship chain with BEST on it.

There was a note too: 'I never gave this to Natalie. Please take it back. It's missed you so much. Amy X.'

Mum read the note over my shoulder. 'Well, I'm glad she's come to her senses.'

I looked up. 'Actually, Mum, I didn't tell you the whole story . . .'

From downstairs came Dad's voice. 'I'll just see your dad off, then you can fill me in,' said Mum.

She left. The chain lay in my hand. I couldn't stop staring at it. It had come back to me so suddenly. It was almost like magic. I blinked away a tear.

'Aaah.'

I started, and looked up.

'Forgotten all about me, hadn't you?' said Jack.

'No, of course not,' I said guiltily. 'These last days you've been such a great friend. It's just a shame you're . . .' I hesitated.

'Imaginary. You can say the word. I won't be offended. Some of the best people have been imaginary. But we can't compete with real people. Once they come on the scene . . . well, you see the results.'

With a shiver of horror I realized I could see right through Jack now. He didn't look real any more.

'You're going, aren't you?'

'Looks like it, yeah. Now, don't forget to hide the tape away, will you?'

'I won't. Jack, I'm really going to miss you.'

You could have hung your washing out on Jack's smile.

And then he was gone.

My bedroom suddenly seemed very empty. I swallowed hard.

But in my hand I still had the friendship chain.

I scrambled out of bed and put it round my neck. It looked just perfect.

Then, remembering Jack's last instructions, I got out my jewellery box. There was a compartment right at the bottom. I put the Creeper tape inside, then locked it away with this tiny key.

I was protecting the Creeper.

For he and Rusty have found that secret hut, and are happy and safe at last.

I'll make certain they are never disturbed again.

THE END

SOME THINGS YOU MAY NOT KNOW ABOUT PETE JOHNSON:

▶▶ He used to be a film critic on Radio One. Sometimes he saw three films a day.

▶▶ He has met a number of famous actors and directors, and collects signed film pictures.

▶▶ Pete's favourite book when he was younger was *One Hundred and One Dalmations*. Pete wrote to the author of this book, Dodie Smith. She was the first person to encourage Pete to be a writer. *Traitor* is dedicated to her.

▶▶ Once when Pete went to a television studio to talk about his books he was mistaken for an actor and taken to the audition room. TV presenter Sarah Greene also once mistook Pete for her brother.

▶▶ When he was younger Pete used to sleepwalk regularly. One night he woke up to find himself walking along a busy road in his pyjamas.

▶▶ Pete's favourite food is chocolate. He especially loves Easter eggs and received over forty this year.

▶▶ Pete's favourites of his own books are *The Ghost Dog* and *How to Train Your Parents*. The books he enjoys reading most are thrillers and comedies.

▶▶ Pete likes to start writing by eight o'clock in the morning. He reads all the dialogue aloud to see if it sounds natural. When he's stuck for an idea he goes for a long walk.

▶▶ He carries a notebook wherever he goes. 'The best ideas come when you're least expecting them' he says.

AVENGER
By Pete Johnson

I can't ever forget what you did! This is war!

Gareth is delighted when Jake, the new boy who's full of
exciting tales befriends him – but when Gareth is caught doing
an impression of Jake's accent, everything changes. Jake is
furious and determined to have his revenge! Gareth has to draw
on the memory of his beloved Grandad, and on the only thing
he has left of him – the magical, mysterious Avenger mask that
Grandad wore when he was a wrestler. But is Jake really the
opponent he seems to be?

A spellbinding thriller about revenge, forgiveness and a very
special friendship, from the hugely popular author of
HOW TO TRAIN YOUR PARENTS:

'The answer to what makes younger teenage boys tick'
TES

'Pete Johnson has created a boy who
makes you laugh out loud.'
Sunday Times

CORGI YEARLING BOOKS
0 440 86458 5